BLOOD IN THE SNOW

The muggers took off running through the snow, which told Longarm they weren't armed with anything more than their knives. He took careful aim at their flying legs. It took two misses before he shot the bigger man in the thigh, causing him to scream. The mugger dropped into the snow with blood spurting from his leg wound.

The smaller man was faster and nearly at the street corner, but Longarm aimed and shot him in the buttocks. The mugger staggered.

"Stop or I'll shoot you again!" Longarm bellowed into the swirling snow. His target ran away.

"Poor, dumb bastard," Longarm muttered, drilling the mugger through the back of his chest.

Longarm ran over to the big man that he'd shot in the thigh. He bent over to help the mugger who promptly drove a knife up at his throat, narrowly missing Longarm's jugular. Then the thug kicked out with his good leg and knocked Longarm to the ground. The wounded man was powerful and he raised his knife, intending to plunge it into Longarm's throat. But Longarm grabbed his attacker's wrist and held the blade away from his body, then slammed his fist into the man's bullet wound.

He went back to the woman they'd assaulted. "Ma'am," he said. "It's over. Are you all right?"

"No, I'm not all right," she said, wiping the snow from her face. "Who *are* you?"

TABOR EVANS

LONGARM
AND "BIG LIPS" LILLY

JOVE BOOKS, NEW YORK

LONGARM AND BIG LIPS LILLY

A Jove Book / published by arrangement with
the author

PRINTING HISTORY
Jove edition / May 2002

Visit our website at
www.penguinputnam.com

ISBN: 0-515-13296-9

A JOVE BOOK®
Jove Books are published by The Berkley Publishing Group,
a division of Penguin Putnam Inc.,
375 Hudson Street, New York, New York 10014.
JOVE and the "J" design
are trademarks belonging to Penguin Putnam Inc.

PRINTED IN THE UNITED STATES OF AMERICA

10 9 8 7 6 5 4 3 2 1

Chapter 1

Deputy Marshal Custis Long stepped into Billy Vail's office and found a chair. Being a relaxed and informal man, Longarm leaned back and placed his heels up on Billy's desk. "I understand you've got a problem in Arizona," he said, glancing outside at a bone-chilling blizzard that was rapidly turning Denver into an ice box.

"As a matter of fact I do."

The blizzard had been raging for two days and had practically paralyzed the city. Longarm was sick and tired of this weather. "I wouldn't mind enjoying some Arizona sunshine."

Marshal Vail was a short, plump man who had once been young, slender and a top field man, like Custis Long. And now, as his eyes also took in the blizzard outside, he wondered if there was any possible way that he could send himself to Arizona instead of his best deputy. There wasn't, of course. Billy had a sweet, equally plump wife and a pair of demanding children who would frown on his absence for more than a day. Also, promotions had bound him to a desk chair for the rest of his government career. But right now, he would have traded everything he owned for some heat, sunshine and a chance to get out of Denver. Like everyone else in the Marshal's Office Federal Building, he was weary of a long, cold winter and fed up with office politics and paperwork.

"I'm not sure what we have in Arizona," Billy began. "Do you remember when that Arizona Territorial Governor Wilder was found murdered in the little railroad town of Williams under strange and mysterious circumstances?"

Custis lit a cheap cheroot. In contrast to Billy Vail, he was a six-foot-four muscular giant. And instead of his skin bearing a white, unhealthy pallor, he was tanned and fit-appearing. "I'm afraid I don't remember that particular murder," he drawled, inhaling deeply. "So why don't you refresh my memory."

"All right," Billy agreed, wrinkling his nose at the stench of Longarm's cigar. "Governor Lance Wilder was quite a politician. Rich, handsome, eloquent and ambitious, he was one of the West's leading political figures. I met him here in Denver a few years back and I never forgot his speech. Governor Wilder had a way of drawing people to his ideas and causes. He was . . . well, almost magnetic."

Longarm wasn't particularly fond of politicians but he supposed there were a few good ones. "I'm sorry I didn't hear his speech. What did he talk about?"

"He had somehow ingratiated himself to no less than James Garfield and was touting his nomination for President. Lance Wilder was also quite a champion of women's suffrage and said that, since women attorneys had recently been given the right to argue cases before the U.S. Supreme Court, they ought to be granted similar rights in all the states and territories."

"Sounds like he was a pretty good man," Longarm said, wondering if he would mind having his legal rights defended by a woman and deciding he would not.

"Governor Wilder was far ahead of his time," Billy

said, wishing that his deputy would buy a better grade of cigar because the stench of those cheap nickel cheroots was nauseating. "Would you mind blowing that cigar smoke in the other direction? I can't even open the windows to air this room out when you leave."

"Why not?"

"Because the frames are frozen shut with ice."

Longarm blew an excellent smoke ring overhead. "Go on about the Governor."

Billy had an excellent memory for crimes, especially the murder of prominent people who, in one way or the other, had something to do with the federal government. Continuing, he said, "Governor Wilder was a bachelor and, from all the newspaper stories I've read, he was a real lady's man. He had mistresses both in Arizona and in Washington. His ambition would have taken him back east where he would have eventually been elected to the U.S. Senate and then possibly even to the presidency. He was that dynamic and talented a politician."

"But he had serious personal flaws," Longarm offered.

"How did you guess?"

"If Wilder was murdered under suspicious circumstances, there must have been a few skeletons in the Arizona governor's closet."

"Yes," Billy confessed, "I'm afraid that there were. You see, Governor Wilder convinced everyone that he had inherited his wealth from an uncle who had gotten his fortune from a mine in Arizona's Superstition Mountains. Only after Wilder's mysterious death was the truth uncovered."

Longarm was getting interested. "And that was?"

"Wilder had once secretly been a professional gambler married to a very successful madam named Big Lips Lilly Cameron."

Longarm's eyebrows shot up. "And he was elected governor?"

"Wilder was quite brilliant," Billy answered. "And I guess the marriage took place before he came to Arizona. Big Lips opened a highly successful string of brothels across Northern Arizona and her girls serviced the workmen building the Atchison, Topeka and Santa Fe Railroad."

"And I suppose that Big Lips serviced them as well?"

"Yes. From what I've heard, she is a striking and intelligent woman who managed to cultivate important people just as easily as did her husband." Billy grinned. "I would think blackmail of some of the more important railroad officials was in order. At any rate, between the profits from her girls and her own conniving, Big Lips and Wilder got rich quick."

"Did she and Governor Wilder ever get divorced?"

"I don't know. Probably not. I mean, they never acknowledged they were married."

"Where is Big Lips now?"

"She was in the Yuma Territorial Prison up until just three months ago."

"What was her crime?"

"She killed two men one night up in Williams, a little town just west of Flagstaff. She claimed it was self defense, but the jury thought otherwise."

"How long did Big Lips serve in prison?"

"Only two years because the men had roughed her up bad."

Longarm turned his attention back to the window. The snow was blowing so hard it flew sideways and the buildings across Colfax Avenue were almost invisible. He could well remember how different it had been during his last warm visit to Yuma in August. "Billy, I've seen the Yuma Prison. Have you?"

"No. Is it really bad?"

"It's not a country club, that's for sure. The most dangerous prisoners are locked in cells blasted out of the

4

adobe and rock with dynamite. They survive like rats in little caves and, in the summer, the temperatures can soar to one hundred and twenty degrees."

"It sounds hellish."

"It is," Longarm agreed. "Even two years in the Yuma prison could make anyone old. Big Lips might not be much to look at today."

"I wouldn't have any idea about that. I've never even seen a picture of the notorious madam," Billy admitted. "But I was fascinated by the secret of her and Governor Wilder. And now, I have a reason to be even more fascinated."

"Go on."

"Big Lips has just been arrested, tried and sentenced to hang for the death of Governor Wilder."

"Did she admit to the murder?"

"Hardly. She maintains that she is innocent and was framed by certain railroad officials who, we can be sure, wish to remain anonymous."

"Obviously so," Longarm said, "but what has all this to do with us?"

"One of the officials that Big Lips has accused of being her former lover and quite possibly the man behind the murder of Governor Wilder is none other than Stanton Pennington."

"Isn't he the . . ."

"Yes," Billy said, cutting Longarm off in mid-sentence. "Stanton Pennington was the vice president of the Atchison, Topeka and Santa Fe and is now Arizona's *new* Territorial Governor."

Longarm chuckled and forgot to blow his smoke aside. A cloud floated across Billy's desk causing his boss to choke and then jump to his feet with indignation. "Dammit, Custis, go put that thing out in the lavatory right now! It's poisonous and I don't know how you can stand to smoke such crap!"

"All right. All right. Calm down."

Longarm did as he was told and when he returned to Billy's office, there was a cloud of noxious blue smoke in the air that he hadn't noticed before. Billy was frantically trying to open the window but, as he'd explained earlier, ice had frozen the window and frame shut.

"Need some help with that?" Longarm offered, wanting to make up for all the bad smoke.

"Sure. Give it a pull but don't break the glass or I'll freeze to death instead of being poisoned by that reeking cheroot."

Longarm figured he was quite a bit stronger than Billy so he gave the window a terrific upward yank. Unfortunately the glass shattered, nearly cutting him as a cold blast of icy air and blowing snow swirled into the office.

"Now look what you've done!" Billy cried.

"Sorry," Longarm said, pulling the shade down. "But I'm sure that this room will now ventilate real well."

Billy swore and ran out into the hallway calling for a building repairman. Longarm watched the flimsy window shade flutter and snow gather on the floor under the broken window. He decided it was probably time to make a quick exit to his own small, cramped but warm office.

"Hey!" Billy shouted as he started down the hallway. "We didn't finish our conversation."

Out of pure orneriness, Longarm said, "It's a little cold in your office, Boss. Why don't you come down to mine and tell me what you expect me to do about Big Lips."

Billy cursed again and followed Longarm to his own cluttered and windowless little cubicle. "Dammit, I don't know why I let you try to unstick that window!"

"Sorry about that," Longarm said, dismissing the subject with a wave of his hand. "Billy, why is it that you want to send me to Northern Arizona concerning a madam and ex-prison inmate who has nothing to do with anything even remotely connected to a federal crime?"

"Oh," Billy said. "I forgot to add that Big Lips is also accused of extorting and then murdering a federal judge."

"I see," Longarm said. "And is Big Lips also saying this federal judge had something to do with the death of her secret husband, the once prominent political genius Lance Wilder?"

"As a matter of fact," Billy replied, "that is exactly what Big Lips is saying."

"When can I escape this freezing weather?"

"As soon as possible."

"That suits me just fine," Longarm told his boss. "It will take me maybe two days to get to warm country where I can thaw."

"Williams, Flagstaff and Prescott are not 'warm country'," Billy reminded him. "They're high up in the mountains."

"That's right," Longarm said, "but their winters sure aren't the equal of ours."

"True," Billy admitted, sounding resentful. "At any rate, this is a complicated situation."

"When is Big Lips Lilly scheduled to hang?"

"In Flagstaff in about a month."

Longarm shook his head. "Billy, we both know that it'll take me at least a full week to get to Arizona! Much longer, if the passes are closed to stage and rail passengers."

"It gives you very little time," Billy said, "but, if Big Lips is guilty of murder, she more than deserves to die. After all, she might just have killed Wilder, the former territorial governor, plus the two other men whom we know nothing about in addition to the federal judge. If so, that adds up to four murders . . . and who knows how many others that Big Lips has managed to hide."

"But she might be innocent of them all," Longarm reminded his boss. "I really don't find it too hard to imagine that she and her secret husband did extort and blackmail

7

prominent judges and railroad officials. But that isn't cause for a hanging."

"No, it isn't." Billy frowned and turned to leave. "I'd better go make sure that someone is on the way up to fix that shattered window. Dammit, Custis, I can't believe that you did that in the middle of a blizzard!"

"I could have done it just as easily on a sunny summer day," Longarm told his irritated boss. "And by the way, how on earth did Miss Lilly Cameron or whatever her real name is get the odd nickname, 'Big Lips'?"

"I don't know, but it sure ought to be interesting finding out."

"Yeah," Longarm said, letting his imagination conjure up all sorts of wonderful possibilities, "it sure will!"

Chapter 2

It took almost an hour for Longarm to get his travel money and paperwork finished. He knew that the Denver and Rio Grande train was pulling out of the depot at one o'clock, so that still gave him several hours to catch the southbound to Pueblo. From there he'd have to get over to Bent's Fort in order to connect with the Atchison, Topeka and Santa Fe line. Longarm knew that the railroad would have a difficult and snowy climb over Raton Pass on its way to Santa Fe, Albuquerque, Gallup and finally Flagstaff and Williams. It wasn't going to be an easy or pleasant train journey, but it was sure better than fighting the elements from the back of a horse or even the inside of a stagecoach.

"You got everything in order?" Billy asked, stepping into Longarm's cubbyhole office just as he was ready to leave.

"Yeah."

"You'll see that I authorized an extra fifty dollars over what you requested." Billy looked his best marshal in the eye. "You may think that you're lucky to be leaving all this cold weather, but you aren't going to an Arizona picnic. This whole business with Big Lips Lilly and the mysterious murders of those others sounds like a can of worms and I honestly feel bad about getting you involved."

"Don't worry," Longarm assured his boss. "I'll sort it all out."

"I hope so. I'm pretty sure that Big Lips is guilty of multiple murders, but we have to make sure. The marshal in Flagstaff has sent me several telegrams detailing the events and he seems to have grave doubts that Big Lips got a fair trail. I guess the people down there are pretty upset with all the murders and intrigue. You know how those small town people think and operate."

"Yeah. They want a quick resolution no matter how complicated the case. And, if the law and the courts can't bring in a guilty verdict, why, they're as likely as not to start talking about a lynching party."

"That's right," Billy said. "So if you should find circumstantial evidence that leads you to think that Big Lips is innocent, you're going to have a lot of local opposition. Furthermore, Big Lips probably has dirt on a good many important people down there who want her silenced . . . permanently."

"This case may take some time."

"You don't have time," Billy countered. "One month and she's history."

"And what if I determine that she's not guilty and need more time to prove it?"

"I don't know what you can do in that case," Billy admitted. "Flagstaff's marshal is named Jessie Conner. He sounds like a good man but that's only a hunch. I hope he can help you."

"Me too." Longarm forced an easy smile. "I wonder if Big Lips *has* big lips?"

"Top or bottom end?" Billy deadpanned.

Longarm couldn't help but laugh, then say, "That's for me to find out and you to wonder about. So long, Billy."

"Good luck. I just hope that your train can get through. If the weather is as bad to the south as it is here in Denver, you might not get over Raton Pass."

Longarm just shrugged to let his friend know that some things were beyond a man's control and just had to be accepted. If the train got stuck in the mountains, his focus would turn to the survival not only of himself, but of the crew and other passengers.

Longarm headed out into the blizzard and then bulled his way through the flying snow and cutting wind to his apartment. He'd need to pack his warmest clothing, making sure he had several pairs of woolen socks and underwear. He owned a big sheepskin-lined leather jacket and some heavy leather boots that were well oiled to keep out the moisture. He'd need a couple pair of heavy-lined gloves and maybe a bottle of rye whiskey just to stave off the bite of cold.

Longarm's preferred sidearm was a double action Colt Model T .44-.40 which he wore on his left hip, butt forward so that it was positioned for the cross draw. But, for insurance, he also had a twin-barreled derringer hideout which was attached by a gold chain to his Ingersol railroad watch. Many times over his career he'd been saved from death by pretending to reach for his watch while in fact going for the derringer.

The Ingersol told him it was time to hurry over to the railroad station and board the southbound. Billy had already sent a messenger to the depot to make his travel arrangements and to pay his fare.

"I just hope the train isn't full," he muttered as he screwed his hat down, opened the door and headed out into the blizzard.

The wind was howling down through the corridors of office buildings and apartments and visibility was almost non-existent. Longarm had about a half mile to go and he knew that no sane carriage operator would be out in this

11

vile weather. That meant he had no choice but to hoof it with his leather suitcase in one gloved fist while his other fist tried to keep his hat from taking flight. His heavy sheepskin-lined coat was buttoned right up to his square jaw and his eyes were watering from the blowing snow and the cold.

The footing was treacherous and Longarm was concentrating so hard on keeping his balance and staying upright that he almost missed seeing the woman just across the street who was being attacked and robbed. The lady had been shoved in a snowbank and was hanging onto her purse for dear life as a pair of street thugs worked her over.

"Hey!" Longarm shouted, jumping into the street and slogging through the deep snow toward the attackers. "Let her go!"

Ordinarily, Denver street muggers were a cowardly lot and when confronted by a man, they'd often just turn tail and run. But this pair were neither the usual drunks or kids that Longarm expected. Instead, they were big bruisers and as Longarm crossed the street, they turned on him and drew knives.

"Mind your own damn business, Mister!" one of them shouted. "Or by gawd we'll cut out your gizzard!"

Longarm looked both ways up and down the street making sure that no one was coming in either direction. It struck him as slightly bizarre that here they were, four total strangers in the middle of a big city and all alone with only their own forthcoming actions determining their fates. Had he not been in such a hurry, he would have been out to arrest this pair and get them to a jail. But, since he was in a hurry and they were obviously determined to rob the woman and maybe beat her to death, his plans needed to be changed.

Longarm dropped his suitcase, removed the glove from his right hand then unbuttoned his coat on the bottom and

12

reached for his Colt revolver. Drawing it out, he pointed at the two men and said, "I'm an officer of the law. Drop the knives and get down on your knees. Do it now!"

Ordinarily, street muggers would have followed his orders. But not this pair. Instead, they grabbed the woman, dragged her out of the snowbank and placed a knife to her throat. Then the largest of the pair pushed the woman out in front of himself and yelled, "You want her to die, go ahead and shoot!"

If the weather had been perfect, Longarm might have granted the man's request for he was quite a bit larger than the poor, battered woman and there was still plenty of target. But the weather wasn't perfect and Longarm knew that he couldn't risk a shot with his watery eyes and the bad visibility. So he holstered his gun and said. "Take her purse and let her go."

They tried, but the woman seemed to have death grip on the purse and wouldn't let it loose. Finally, the smaller of the men punched her in the stomach so hard that she doubled up and then he struck her behind the ear and she dropped into the snow, finally releasing the purse.

"You can have her now!" the bigger man shouted, a triumphant leer on his face. "We got what we want."

They made a bad mistake when they turned and started to run away. Longarm drew his gun and shouted one last warning. "Halt or I'll shoot!"

The muggers took off running which told Longarm they weren't armed with anything more than their knives. If they'd have had guns, they were nervy enough to have risked a deadly shoot-out.

Longarm took careful aim at their flying legs making sure that there was nothing but a brick wall as a background and then he began to fire. It took two misses before he shot the bigger man in the thigh, causing him to emit a scream that would have done a mountain lion proud. The man dropped into the snow with blood spurting from his leg wound.

The smaller man was faster and nearly to the corner of the street so Longarm knew that he had an excellent chance to escape. Unwilling to allow that to happen, he raised his sight and shot the man in the buttocks. The mugger staggered, desperate to reach the safety of the corner. Longarm saw the blood staining the back of his pants.

"Stop or I'll shoot you again!" he bellowed into the swirling wind.

The man twisted around, eyes wide and confused. He screamed something, probably a curse, then staggered on, still bent on escape.

"Poor, dumb bastard," Longarm muttered, drilling the man through the back of his chest and sending his body skidding onto the snow-covered sidewalk.

Longarm ran over to the big man that he'd shot in the thigh. He bent over to help the mugger who promptly drove a knife up at his throat, narrowly missing the jugular. Then the thug kicked out with his good leg and knocked Longarm to the ground. The Colt in his cold hand was knocked loose and it plunged into the snow half buried. The wounded man was powerful and he raised his knife intending to plunge it into Longarm's throat. Longarm grabbed the man's wrist and held the blade away from his body wishing that he'd aimed higher and killed this mad man instead of trying to only wound him. They were of equal size and strength and, for a moment, the outcome was in serious doubt. But then Longarm slammed his fist into the man's bullet wound. The mugger screamed in agony and Longarm broke his nose with his closed fist, threw the big man aside and dove into the snow seeking his revolver.

"You son of a bitch!" the wounded man cried, attacking again with his knife.

Longarm's nearly frozen fingers located his gun. He swung it up and fired in one smooth motion only an instant before he would have been fatally stabbed. His bullet struck the mugger between the eyes and blew out the back of his head.

Panting and feeling as if he'd just fought a grizzly, Longarm holstered his gun and climbed to his feet, eyes fixed on the dead man and the pool of dark blood now coloring the snow.

"I'll give you this," he said, retrieving the victim's purse. "You thieves were mighty determined."

He went over to the dazed woman and took a handful of snow and pressed it to her battered face. "Ma'am," he said, "it's over. I had to kill both of them. Are you all right?"

"No, I'm not all right," she said, wiping the snow from her face and staring up at him with little or no comprehension. "Who *are* you?"

One of her eyes was nearly closed and her cheeks were badly bruised. Her lips were puffy and smeared with blood but, otherwise, she seemed to be in good shape.

"I'm a United States Marshal," he said, not bothering to dig out his badge. "And, if that ever happens again, my advice to you would be to hand over your purse. It's not worth losing your life for."

"Yes, it is," she said, hugging the purse to her body. "You don't have any idea what's inside."

"Whatever it is, it's not worth dying for."

"It was to me," she told him. "It's all the money I own in the world."

Longarm wasn't in any mood to argue. He still had a train to catch and it was still blowing a blizzard. "I'll help you to shelter," he said. "We need to get off the streets."

"I was on my way to the train depot," she told him, as she climbed unsteadily to her feet. "I'd just come from the bank and I was going to board the train. I didn't think anyone would dare come out in this weather."

"Did they know you were carrying a lot of money?"

"Maybe." The woman wiped blood from her split lips. "If fact, they did know. One of them was at the bank when I cashed the check and put the money in my purse."

"Then that explains why they were so fixed on getting that purse even when I gave them a first warning."

"Yes," she said. "But can we continue on with this discussion once we are on the train? I'm beaten, bloodied and freezing."

"Of course," he said. "How far are you going?"

"All the way to Arizona."

"So am I."

"That's nice. If I get mugged on the train, maybe you'll be around to save my life and money again."

"Maybe," he said, "but you shouldn't count on it. It's unwise for anyone to carry a lot of cash."

She didn't like being lectured and it showed when she took his arm to steady herself and said, "Let's go."

"I should tell someone about these bodies."

Longarm went to the nearest store, a small bakery and quickly explained what had happened outside. "Just let the authorities know that those two thieves were shot to death by a United States marshal named Custis Long. They know me and that I wouldn't shot to kill unless it was a matter of life or death."

The bakery store owner, a short, balding man with a large paunch and chubby red cheeks, got excited and exclaimed, "You mean there are two dead men lying out there in the snow?"

"That's right. But they won't be causing anyone any more trouble. All you have to do is tell the local authorities what I said and they'll handle everything."

The baker started to ask more questions but Longarm hurried back outside into the blowing snow. The woman was gone but her tracks were still plain and it was obvious

16

that she was headed for the train depot. Longarm hurried after her thinking that she was being pretty inconsiderate to abandon him after he'd killed two men to save her life and fortune. But then, he reasoned that she was simply impatient and he'd catch up with her at the train station or, if not, he'd run into her on the train itself.

He also wondered what she'd look like if her face hadn't been battered and bruised. Pretty, he'd bet.

He searched for his hat but it couldn't be found. No doubt it had sailed off down the street and someone else would benefit from his misfortune. The brown, flat-brimmed Stetson had cost him plenty and was almost new. He wondered if the woman going to Arizona would offer to buy him a replacement if she knew she had cost him his good Stetson.

After all, that was a small price in exchange for her life and fortune.

Chapter 3

Longarm didn't see the young woman whose money and perhaps life he'd saved. The train was nearly empty in the second-class coach where he was riding and that was good because it meant he could stretch out on the bench seats and catch some sleep.

"Afternoon, Marshal. Are you going far?" the conductor asked as he stoked the potbellied stove to heat the coach.

"I'm afraid so. Got to go down to Bent's Fort, then catch the Atchison, Topeka and Santa Fe to Arizona."

"That's going to be quite a feat in this weather. I hope you're not in a big hurry. I've heard that the snows are pretty deep going over Raton Pass as well as up near Flagstaff."

"I'll just have to take my chances."

Longarm spread his coat on the bench and noted that there were only three other second-class passengers, a middle-aged man wearing an ill-fitting and rumpled suit and tie, his wife and a good-looking boy about twelve years old. They were poor folks from the looks of their worn clothing and cheap suitcases. They also had a flimsy wicker basket full of bread and a large jug of either water or wine. Longarm could see wet newspaper hanging through big holes in the bottoms of their shoes and he hoped that the weather was better wherever they were bound.

"Going far?" Longarm asked, wanting to be friendly with his fellow traveling companions.

The short but stocky and handsome man with the long handlebar mustache smiled and nodded vigorously but didn't reply. His wife smiled too but it wasn't pretty because her front teeth were crooked and darkly stained. The boy stared at Longarm, reflecting neither friendliness nor hostility. He was going to be a handsome man with enormous almond-colored eyes and thick, curly black hair.

"They're immigrants," the conductor leaned over and whispered. "Greeks, Sicilians or maybe Italians. They don't speak any English and I had a hell of a time trying to figure out their destination."

"Where are they going?" Longarm asked.

"All the way to San Francisco. I hope they have the money to buy more bread and wine. Those few loaves they have stuffed in that picnic basket won't hold them long in this cold weather."

"We got plenty of coal for the stove, don't we?"

"Enough to get us to Santa Fe. And, if we run out we can always stop and chop some firewood."

Longarm was satisfied with that answer. He heard the train whistle's loud blast and then felt the jerk of the car as it broke its inertia. "Say," he drawled, "did a young woman with a bruised and puffy face get on board?"

"Medium height with a brown coat and long hair?"

"That would be the one."

"Yeah," the conductor said. "She has a private compartment in the first-class coach. First time I saw her I wondered if she was all right or not. She looked like she'd gotten smacked hard in the face a couple times."

"Two thugs tried to rob her but she wouldn't let them

have her purse," Longarm said. "Happened right out there in the middle of downtown but no one was watching. If I hadn't just happened along, no telling what would have become of her."

"Did you arrest the damned muggers?"

"No time for that, so I shot them both to death."

The conductor's jaw dropped. "You killed 'em?"

"That's right. Actually, they gave me no choice. One of them almost managed to get his knife into me."

"Good riddance. What kind of men would beat up a pretty young woman like that?"

"They were after her money," Longarm said.

"Well," the conductor added, "I have a feeling that young lady is pretty well off. I see a lot of passengers from all walks of life and I have gotten so I can judge people. That young woman was a mess but she was wearing very expensive clothing. Her boots were wet and muddy but I recognized the maker and he doesn't sell his goods cheap."

"Did she give you her name?"

"Yes. Miss Hanson."

"Do me a favor," Longarm mused, "and watch out for her. She had quite a fight and gave a good account of herself. She's small but there's nothing weak about the young lady."

The conductor nodded and finished stoking the stove. "There's more coal in the box," he said to the immigrant and his family, then he made it clear that they were to shovel it into the potbelly if they got cold.

Longarm watched the blowing snow through his window and caught snatches of Denver before he stretched out on the seat, laid his head on his baggage and went to sleep.

He awoke several hours later to see the immigrant family having a small meal of their bread and wine. It was still snowing hard and it took him awhile to realize they had a ways to go before they reached Pueblo. Longarm had forgotten to eat before leaving Denver and maybe it showed because the man motioned for him to join them.

"No thanks," Longarm said. "I'll just go up to the dining car and have a bite to eat. Appreciate the offer, though."

He hesitated only a minute, wondering if he dared to leave his belongings unattended. He didn't really want to haul his baggage through the coaches, and he did not want to insult this poor family by making it clear they weren't worthy of being trusted.

"I'll just leave my things right here and be back in a while," he told them, pointing to his own modest suitcase.

Longarm realized his clothes had gotten soiled in the street fight and he looked kind of rough. Still, there wasn't any place to change and he guessed he'd better save his clean duds for Flagstaff; once there he could send the dirty clothes he was wearing to a Chinese laundry.

Passing through the cars on his way forward, he saw the entire train was nearly empty. It seemed most people had better things to do than to attempt travel during a snowstorm.

"Marshal?" the conductor asked when he entered the dining car. "I don't think it would matter if you took a compartment in this first-class coach. I mean, it's not going to hurt anybody or deprive the railroad of income and we are carrying gold and cash in the mail coach safe that are bound for the San Francisco mint. There is an armed guard watching over that bullion, but having you on board gives us an extra degree of comfort and security."

"I'd be be much obliged," Longarm said, delighted by this news. In a first-class coach he could get far more sleep and rest.

"Think nothing of it," the conductor told him. "You'll be in compartment number three right next to that young Miss Hanson in number two. I figured, after what she

21

went through, she'd be comforted to sleep near a lawman."

"How long will it be until we reach Pueblo?"

"A couple more hours."

Longarm went back and retrieved his baggage, waving good-bye to the immigrants who seemed to regret his departure. Feeling a bit guilty for leaving them all by themselves and enjoying what he really wasn't paying for, Longarm said, "You folks have the whole coach to yourselves now so just take it easy and keep feeding that stove and stay warm."

He carried his things up to compartment number three. Then, with his belly still growling, he went to the little dining car where he saw Miss Hanson sitting alone at a table. There wasn't another passenger in the car and she looked sad and maybe a bit uncomfortable because of her appearance.

"Hi," he said, reaching up to remove his Stetson then remembering it had blown away in downtown Denver. "Would you mind a little company?"

She shook her head, then offered her hand. "My name is Irene Hanson, and I'm sorry that I left you back in Denver but I simply *had* to get on board this train."

"I figured as much. How are you feeling?"

She had bathed, combed her hair and applied some makeup to disguise the worst of the purplish bruises on her cheeks, but nothing could have hidden the puffy shiners around both eyes.

"I'm feeling much better now," she said. "And I am also feeling a bit ashamed of myself for not thanking you properly. You not only saved me . . . but also my money."

"It was my pleasure."

"I find that hard to believe. After all, you were nearly killed and you wound up shooting two men to death. And I suspect you have a few aches, pains and bruises of your own."

22

"I was wearing my thick leather coat so I didn't get hurt as much as you might think," Longarm confessed. "And as for the two men that I had to shoot, I don't feel good about that, but they were cowards without conscience to prey on a single woman. They were beating you like a man and I sure don't feel sorry for sending them to their just reward in hell."

"Can I buy you dinner?"

"I can pay for my own," he said. "Even at the railroad's prices."

"It is expensive," she agreed. "But I owe you everything. Please let me buy you drinks and dinner."

Longarm was a gentlemen and the idea of a woman paying went against his grain. On the other hand, it was obvious that Irene really wanted to do this in repayment and she obviously had far more money than himself so he said, "I'd appreciate that as long as you don't expect any special favors, Miss."

It was meant as a joke but it fell flat. "I'd never expect any special favors, Marshal. This is a repayment, not a bribe for your continued protection."

"Only kidding," he said, signaling for a drink.

"I'm actually from Texas," she told him after ordering a bottle of excellent whiskey and filling their glasses. "But I moved to Arizona about four years ago with my husband, Charlie Hanson."

"You're married?"

"I'm a widow."

"I see."

"My late husband owned a freighting company down in Prescott, Arizona. Eighteen months ago he was transporting some ore and expensive merchandise when he was ambushed. The coroner and physician who examined his body said that he died instantly from a bullet to the brain."

"I'm very sorry."

"Charlie was a good husband and a good man," Irene

23

said, swallowing hard. "I can't say that we were in love, but we did respect each other and we were the best of friends."

"Did you love him when you were first married?"

"I *liked* him," Irene said, emphasizing the word. "We had known each other since childhood. You know, Marshal, sometimes *liking* is more important than loving." She looked closely at him. "Does it surprise you to hear me say that?"

"A little," he admitted.

"Do you have lady friends?"

"Oh yes, quite a few."

"I can believe that." She emptied her glass and poured more whiskey. "And do you think that you can remain friends with those ladies without . . . well, you know?"

Even with her bruised cheeks he could see that Irene was blushing. "You know what?" he asked, hating himself for putting her on the spot and making her squirm a bit.

"Without . . . making love to them!"

Longarm stroked his thick handlebar mustache. "That's a hard thing to say, Mrs. Hanson. I mean, when you like a woman, you often want to take it to the next step and fall in love with her and then make love to her with great passion."

Irene rested her chin on the back of her wrist and studied him closely. "But what if you liked a woman as a friend and found her physically unappealing? Would you still want to make love to her?"

Longarm decided this conversation was getting deep pretty fast and he would have liked to dodge the question but she was pinning him with her intense blue eyes and he felt he should at least attempt to give her an honest answer.

"If she was unappealing, married or involved with another man and I found myself thinking romantic thoughts of her, then I'd probably decide that I need to put some distance between us."

"So you'd end the friendship because the woman was homely?"

Longarm scowled and took a deep swallow of whiskey. He wasn't sure if he appreciated the direction of this conversation, but she was paying for the whiskey and dinner so he did his best to hold up his end.

"Mrs. Hanson, I do have some longtime homely women friends that I hold very dear. But when I meet an attractive and unattached young woman like you . . . then I admit to some . . . stirrings."

"Stirrings of the heart?" Her lips held a faint smile.

"Stirrings of the heart and profound stirrings in another place," he said, looking her square in the eye.

"I see." Irene took a deep breath and expelled it slowly. "Well, Marshal, I appreciate your candor. Yes, I certainly do."

"Thank you."

"And," she continued, "I am very aware that men and women are quite different. I know that from being married and . . . from earlier experiences with men."

"You don't have to explain anything to me." Longarm refilled both their glasses. "Mrs. Hanson, may I say that I hold you in the highest possible regard? You are not only a brave and determined woman, but also a very lovely and desirable one."

She blushed even more deeply and raised her glass. "How far did you say you were going?"

"About as far as you are."

"Hmmm, I think that this is going to be a much more interesting and pleasant journey than I could have possibly imagined."

"I share that exact sentiment."

Their dinner came and it was excellent. Irene ordered a bottle of wine and asked the waiter to put what was left of their whiskey in a bag along with two glasses. Longarm thought that was a very promising sign.

"Marshal?"

"Why don't you call me Custis."

"All right. Have you ever been married?"

He was instantly on guard. "Nope."

"Why not?"

"My job isn't one that lends itself well to the institution of holy matrimony."

They were both a little drunk and Irene's words were slightly slurred, but she hadn't lost her earlier intensity. "But you *could* quit your job and find a safer line of work, couldn't you?"

"Yes, but I don't want to."

"Dear Charlie felt the same way about his freighting business. He'd made enough money to hire teamsters for every run, but he loved driving those mules over the mountain roads. He was a fine muleskinner and took pride in that line of work. I did the books and scheduling and we made a great team. Charlie wouldn't have had it any other way."

"Neither would I," Longarm told her. Then he told her about his boss, Billy Vail, and ended up by saying, "Billy is a few years past his prime but he still says the best time of his life was when he held my job. When he was free and when there was danger, which is the real spice of life."

"But he married and took the desk job?"

"That's right. And there are times when I go over to his house and see what a fine table his wife sets and how his children are reasonably well-behaved and give him great pride and satisfaction. Then I say to myself, 'Custis, this looks pretty good. He makes more money than you. He doesn't risk his life and he has a wife and children to come home to every night. A warm house, a loving family and good, hot meals to enjoy. And what do you have?

26

Just a little apartment that looks like it ought to be condemned and you eat out most every night or cook something that a goat would refuse' "

Irene laughed. "A goat? Is bachelorhood really that bad?"

"No," he admitted, "but compared to a man with a good wife and children, it can be lonely and lean. Still, I'm not complaining."

"You shouldn't be," she told him. "I'm quite sure that you could easily find a sweet and beautiful bride who would be very happy being Mrs. Custis Long."

Longarm poured them the last of the wine and raised his glass with a sly grin. "Irene, how can you say that, given my slovenly housekeeping and dangerous life style?"

"I say it because you are obviously a good man. And one that is . . . well, forgive me for being so bold . . . very chivalrous and handsome."

"Shall we turn in?' he asked.

"Yes, I think we should." Irene laid her money on the fine tablecloth linen. "We've certainly had a wonderful dinner and conversation."

He collected the still half-full bottle of whiskey as they prepared to leave the dining car. "It sure doesn't have to end here and now."

Irene shivered. "No, it doesn't."

Even with her swollen eyes and lips, the woman possessed a red-hot sensuality that caused Longarm to feel that profound stirring he had alluded to earlier. So he followed her out of the dining car and into the first-class coach with its individual compartments.

"Yours or mine?" he asked.

"Yours, of course."

Longarm didn't see why Irene thought the choice should have been obvious but again, that was one of those fundamental differences between men and women that he

27

occasionally failed to divine. And anyway, it didn't matter because he knew the outcome.

Their space was limited but they made themselves comfortable. Because the coach was divided into compartments, it tended to be chilly so they had another glass of whiskey then dove under a pile of woolen blankets after shedding only their below-the-waist clothing and undergarments.

"This is going to be pretty elemental, isn't it?" Irene asked as she spread her legs wide apart.

"We've both had a hard day and we're each pretty banged up," he explained. "So why don't we do what we want to do and then get some rest and save the finer points for later?"

"I can't even kiss you, my lips are so painful." Irene reached under the covers and grabbed his thick manhood. "But I think this will certainly be a wonderful distraction."

She guided his thick root into her womanhood then pulled him close whispering, "Just hold me for a few moments and let the rocking of the train give us slow and sweet pleasure."

Longarm buried his face into her hair. "You smell good. I didn't even take a bath. I not only eat food unfit for a goat, but I smell like one."

"You were ticketed for the second-class coach. There are no baths to be had back there."

"How do you know?" he asked, feeling a tingling in his toes.

"Because I've been poor most of my life. I knew you were back there and I wanted to reward your services, so here you are."

Longarm raised up and looked down at her with surprise. "You mean you paid for me to come up here in this coach?"

"Certainly. Do you think the railroad gave you first-class fare just because they are generous?"

"But the conductor said they have gold and valuables in the safe and. . . ."

Irene drew him close, reaching out to cup his hard buttocks with both hands. By pulling him deeper and thrusting her hips vigorously, Longarm knew that she was already approaching the point where the gentle rocking of the coach wasn't good enough. The woman wanted a good, hard session of lovemaking.

"Oh, Custis, use me harder!" she gasped as her passion intensified. "Let's try to do this all the way to Arizona!"

"That's fine with me," he panted, feeling as if he were going to erupt like a volcano.

Irene buried her face in his neck and began to squeal with pleasure. Pistoning his big rod in and out and then around, Longarm soon had the woman thrashing in ecstasy and milking his body of every drop of his spurting seed.

"Oh, you're so good," Irene panted, trying to catch her breath. "I sure as hell wish we were both going all the way to San Francisco."

"It doesn't have to end when we reach Arizona."

"I'm afraid that it does," she said. "But let's just make every minute we have together one to remember."

Longarm thought that was probably for the best. And besides, he needed to keep his mind on Big Lips Lilly Cameron and learn if she should live . . . or die.

Chapter 4

They had switched trains at Bent's Fort on the Arkansas River and Irene must have paid the railroad extra fare because Longarm again found himself enjoying first-class accommodations. The blizzard had passed, but snow was still falling and there was at least three feet of snow on the countryside. And, as the train climbed, following the old Santa Fe Trail, everyone was wondering how bad things might be at Raton Pass.

"Did you hear anything on the wire at Bent's Fort?" Longarm asked the conductor once they were rolling south again.

"The telegraph is down somewhere between Trinidad and Raton," the man answered. "Our engineer made the decision to steam on to Trinidad and hope we can find out more about the pass."

"How bad can it be?" Irene asked as they sat in the dining car having breakfast.

"Real bad," the conductor answered. "We hope that the railroad has sent a locomotive up there ahead of us with a snow plow to clear the tracks, but you can never be sure. And sometimes, if it's snowing hard enough, the track can be cleared then covered again in just an hour or two. That's happened on my watch just once and I thought we were going to freeze to death."

Irene looked to Longarm, then back at the conductor. "So what happened when you got stuck?"

"They hooked up a pair of locomotives in Raton with a big snow blade on the front and bulled their way up to us. Then we followed them back down and got out of the pass okay."

"That sounds pretty bad," Irene said.

"It was scary, but we had enough coal and food in this dining car to keep us well fed and warm so we didn't suffer," the conductor assured her. "But that shouldn't happen again. We'll be stopping in Trinidad to take on more coal and water. That's where I expect we'll finally get some news about the pass. If they believe that it's snowed under, then we'll stay in Trinidad for however long it takes."

Longarm kept his silence. They'd boarded about two dozen new passengers at Pueblo and Bent's Fort, so there were now maybe thirty-five or forty passengers in addition to the train crew. And while he sure didn't want any delays, there was no sense in fretting about something that was beyond his control.

Finishing his meal, he excused himself. "Irene, I think I'll go back to the mail car and see how the guard is getting along. My services aren't going to be wanted or needed, but I'd still like to know what kind of security is guarding the safe and its contents."

"I understand," she said. "I'm going back to my compartment. You know where to find me."

"I sure do."

Longarm visited the mail car which was little more than an oversized ice box without insulation. Pikes, picks, axes, snow shovels and other heavy tools rested in a large metal box while crates of emergency train parts were stacked to

31

the ceiling; an icy wind whistled through open cracks in the walls. Other than the mountains of snow-dusted crates, there was nothing else except a safe that was wrapped in chains and padlocked, a few chairs, a potbellied stove and one half-frozen security guard.

The poor, shivering fellow was bundled up so heavily against the cold that he couldn't have drawn his gun in less than a minute. Not that Longarm blamed him because of the numbing temperature.

"My name is Marshal Custis Long. How are you doing?"

"I'm freezing my butt off!" the guard stuttered, steam clouds issuing from his mouth with every word. "I've been here for six solid hours without a break and I'm about to say the hell with it and quit this miserable job!"

Longarm went over to the stove and placed his hand on its rusty side to feeling its dying warmth. "Don't you have any more fuel for this stove?"

"They gave me a box of coal when we left Denver but it's long gone. I figure they'll replenish it in Trinidad." The man slapped his gloved hands together, then vigorously rubbed his thick beard. He was in his thirties, lean and hatchet-faced with close-set, sad brown eyes. "Say, Marshal, suppose you can talk the conductor into giving me some extra coal right now?"

"I'll try," Longarm promised. "We're still fifty miles north of Trinidad and the going is only going to get worse."

"I know. I've been on this run more times than I care to count. And I'll tell you another thing . . . if the snow is this deep down here in the lower country, you can bet it's going to be at least three times as deep on top of Raton Pass."

"What is the matter with that old safe?"

"Someone either lost or forgot the combination, so they just chain it up with a padlock."

Longarm shook his head. "That's pathetic. I'll go and talk to the conductor right now."

"It's not the railroad's responsibility," the guard explained. "The company I work for—Colorado Security—is the one at fault. They keep telling us guards that they've ordered a new safe, but I know better. A new safe that size will cost them more than a thousand dollars and they just don't have the money."

Longarm inspected the chain. It was stout but certainly not a substitute for a working safe. "When I get to Trinidad, maybe I'll have a talk with your boss."

"Too late," the guard said. "Their office is back in Pueblo. And it wouldn't help even if you did tell them that they need a new safe. I'm pretty sure that Colorado Security is going broke. That's why I'm quitting. A man can only take so much abuse and then he needs to walk away and hunt for something better to do with his life. I used to be a cowboy but I got kicked in the knee cap. It lamed me up for keeps. If I was a horse, they'd have shot me. Now, I got a leg so bum I can't even stand for more than an hour or so at a time and I can't sit in a saddle."

Longarm nodded with sympathy, realizing that this guard was fit only to sit in a chair and, since he was probably unable to read or write, this was one of the few jobs he could hold. "What's your name?"

"Jack Slater. I live in Santa Fe with my mother who is in poor health. My father died about three years ago. He had lost his mind and he finally just wandered out in a snow storm; we found him frozen as hard as a bent railroad spike. I've been sitting here wondering if I was going to share the same poor fate."

Slater banged his gloves together. "I'm feeling real bad, Marshal. You wouldn't happen to have a little whiskey to warm my poor innards, would you?"

"No, but I'll tell the conductor to bring you some coal

for that stove along with some hot coffee. It's freezing in here."

"You ain't tellin' me anything I don't already know."

"I'll be right back," Longarm promised.

"Hey, I sure wouldn't mind if the coffee was laced with some tarantula juice, if you know what I mean!"

Longarm knew what Slater meant, but figured that, since the man was still on the job, he shouldn't be drinking. Custis made his way up to the dining car and requested that the conductor give Jack Slater more coal and some coffee.

"Slater doesn't work for the railroad and we're not supposed to give the guards anything for free."

"But the poor devil is freezing to death!"

"I'm truly sorry about that. I know Jack Slater and he's a decent enough man although he never bathes and he can get ornery when he drinks. Still and all, no man deserves to sit in that mail car for hours on end in this kind of foul weather. But I just do my job like the railroad tells me. I'm only supposed to take care of the *paying* passengers. Now, if Jack wants to buy some extra coal and coffee, then. . . ."

Longarm dug into his pocket for money because Slater didn't have two nickels to rub together. The ex-cowboy was probably being paid almost nothing by Colorado Security for his risk and suffering. "Here," he said, handing the conductor a silver dollar. "Give Jack more coal, a hot meal and some coffee."

The conductor studied the coin resting in the palm of his hand then gave it back to Longarm. "I'm a Christian man and it isn't right to let another man suffer. So to hell with the railroad's rules! I'll just let them pay for the coal, the meal and Jack's coffee. And I'll deliver it to poor Slater with a smile."

Longarm was pleased and said, "That's the spirit! And by the way, are you aware that the safe is broken?"

34

"Sure. The company that contracted to guard the valuables is about to go under. Until they do, however, there's little that can be done to improve the situation."

"I see. How is that immigrant family in second-class?"

"I finally figured out they are from Italy. Unfortunately, some fellas got on in Pueblo and were giving that family lots of grief, but I told them to behave themselves. It's not right to haze and cuss out those kind of poor folks that come from other countries."

"Who was giving them trouble?"

"They're miners or lumberman, I'd guess. Anyway, they were drunk when they boarded and they brought whiskey onto the train. All three decided that making fun of Italians is great sport."

Longarm's jaw muscles knotted. "I'll go back and have a word with them. That's a nice family. They look like they've gone through a lot to get this far and I don't much cotton to the notion that anyone should be giving them a bad time."

"I agree, but you know how some men are when they've had too much to drink."

"Yeah," Longarm said, his lips tight with anger. "I sure do."

When he entered the second-class coach the three troublemakers were howling with laughter and one of them had a thick finger pointed at the Italian father whose hands were clasped together. His wife sat close beside him and she looked up at Longarm with a plea in her dark eyes. The boy was pale and his lips formed a hard, tight line across his handsome face. Longarm saw anger and defiance there and knew that, if the boy had been a man, he would not have allowed his family to be subjected to so much abuse.

Walking up to the three men, Longarm unbuttoned his coat so that the butt of his Colt stood out prominently.

He hooked his thumbs in his gun belt and said, "You boys have some little joke you want to share?"

All three turned their faces up to Longarm and one of them said, "We think that people who can't speak English ought to be tarred and feathered or . . . or hanged!"

To emphasize his point, the man lifted both hands as if he were hanging onto a rope that was affixed around his neck and then he stuck his tongue out and made gagging sounds.

His companions thought their friend's little charade hilarious and began to howl.

Longarm wanted to crack their heads with the heavy barrel of his six-gun and he was so furious that it was all that he could do to keep his voice steady when he said, "I'm a United States marshal and I think you boys have had about enough to drink. Furthermore, I'm going to warn you just once that I won't tolerate your hazing that family or anyone else on this train. So sit still, shut up and keep quiet."

They stopped laughing. One of them fumbled at his coat pocket and finally dragged out a bottle of whiskey. "Marshal, huh? Well how about a drink on old Dirk Jones!"

The man started to upend the bottle and Longarm let him have a swallow before he slammed the bottle down into the man's throat. It went in several inches and caused the man to choke and try to pull it out. Longarm didn't allow that to happen. Instead, he jammed the bottle even deeper and his victim's eyes bugged and whiskey poured out of the corners of his mouth.

The other two men reached for something and Longarm figured it wouldn't be whiskey so he drew his gun and did what he'd wanted to do from the moment he'd entered second-class and that was to pistol-whip the braying fools. He hit them both so hard and fast they didn't have time to drag up their six-guns before they collapsed, instantly unconscious.

Returning his attention to his first victim, Longarm finally retracted the bottle of whiskey and used it as a club.

"I don't think these fellas will be bothering you folks anymore," he told the Italian family as well as the other amazed passengers. "And when we get to Trinidad, I'm going to see that these boys get the boot."

"But they bought tickets all the way to Raton," one of the passengers stammered. "I overheard them saying they had jobs waiting at some timber mill on the far side of Raton Pass."

Longarm shrugged with indifference. "Maybe I'll let them go that far just in case we get stuck and need someone extra hands to man snow shovels. If these boys were sober, they could probably do the work."

"When they wake up, they might just decide to shoot us all and be done with it," the man said. "Marshal, you can't just leave them here to wake up and then take it out on us!"

The man was scared, and with some justification. Longarm had been so angry that he'd cracked all three of them with more than the required force. He might even have inflicted some permanent damage, although he thought they were such hard-headed louts that they'd fully recover.

"I just hate bullies," he said, looking over at the Italian boy and seeing a faint smile on the kid's face. "I guess you find them all over the world, huh? Every culture, every race. Doesn't matter."

The boy didn't understand a word he said, but that didn't matter because now the kid was smiling and so were his parents, although they were trying to keep straight faces.

"What are you going to do, Marshal?" the frightened man persisted.

Longarm frowned. "Well, I guess I could arrest them for creating a disturbance, but I don't have three pairs of handcuffs nor do I have any rope."

"Well you can't. . . ."

Longarm cut the man off. "So I think what I'm going to do is ask some of you men to pick them up and carry their worthless carcasses to the mail car where they'll be easy to watch. So Mister, you and some of the other men, get over here and lend a hand."

"We didn't buy tickets expecting to have to work. I got a bad back, Marshal and. . . ."

"Quit whining and get over here!" Longarm commanded.

The man jumped up showing no physical problems and so did several other men. The Italian and his son also came to their feet and lent strong, helping hands.

"Jack," Longarm said, as they arrived with the three inert loggers who were tossed to the floor. "You're gonna have some company over the pass."

Slater jumped out of his chair and gaped at the three men who all had blood streaks on their faces from having their skulls severely indented.

"What the hell!"

"Troublemakers," Longarm snapped. "They couldn't behave themselves in the second-class coach so they're going to spend the rest of their trip right here with you."

Slater shook his head. "Now wait a minute, Marshal. I don't get paid for guarding hard cases."

"I know and the conductor doesn't get paid for bringing you extra coal for your stove . . . by the way, it's a lot warmer in here now . . . isn't it?"

"Why sure! But. . . ."

"And I see you've got a full urn of piping hot coffee. Now Jack, I bet that warmed up your innards, didn't it?"

"Yeah, Marshal, but . . ."

"So I know that you're feeling grateful and you won't mind these three lying on the floor here."

"Well what if they wake up before we get to Trinidad and want to take things out on me?"

"What you need to do then is just tap them firmly on their skulls like I did and I guarantee they'll go right back to sleep."

"You mean pistol-whip 'em?"

"That's right."

Jack was on his feet and now he pushed back the woolen cap on his head and scratched his thin hair. "Marshal, I ain't used to doin' that sort of thing. I'd be afraid of maybe hitting at least one of 'em too hard and maybe killing him or doing him permanent harm."

"It is a gamble," Longarm said. "But so is everything else in life. Just give it a try and I'll be checking up on you every half hour or so. I'll even bring you more coffee if you run out."

"I dunno."

"One good turn deserves another, Jack. So be a good man and do as I tell you."

Longarm turned to the door. All his helpers except the Italian kid had gone back to second-class. "Send this one up through the cars to first-class if things get out of hand."

Jack looked at the kid. "What's his name?"

"I don't know. He doesn't speak English yet."

"My name Antonio Russo," the boy said in clear but halting English. "How do you do?"

"I do fine," Longarm replied. "My name is Marshal Custis Long. Pleased to meet you and your family."

Antonio's smile widened. "I help more?"

Longarm motioned toward the three unconscious lumbermen and then he stepped over to the tool box and found a spare axe handle. Hefting it, Longarm walked over to the three men lying on the floor and made it very clear what was to be done if they awakened and became

39

belligerent. Then he handed the axe handle to Antonio instead of Jack. The Italian kid grinned even wider.

"Well, Jack," Longarm said. "I think it's clear that you have been relieved of the responsibility of busting their skulls. Young Antonio Russo seems to like the idea of assuming that job."

"You're gonna let *him* whack 'em?"

"If necessary," Longarm said, winking at the Italian and then leaving the coach.

On his way through the cars, he glanced out the windows. It had begun to snow again, making him think that getting over Raton Pass was going to be one hell of a challenge.

Chapter 5

It was still snowing when they pulled into Trinidad, a ranching and railroad town deep in southern Colorado. The conductor hustled down the aisle shouting, "Ninety minute layover. Everyone who wants, prepare to disembark."

Longarm had been resting but now he knocked on Irene's door and called, "Do you want to get some fresh air?"

"No thanks," she said, opening the door to her compartment. "It looks terrible out there."

"It doesn't look good. I need to find the telegraph office and send a message back to Denver. Anything you want while I'm in town?"

"We might need more whiskey."

"Good idea. We might get stranded on Raton Pass and we sure don't want to run out of liquor."

Longarm paid a quick visit to the mail car. Jack Slater was waiting and impatient to leave. "I'm quitting, so what are you going to do with these three fellas that you pistol-whipped?"

"Where is the Italian boy?"

"I sent him on back to stay with his family."

Longarm wasn't pleased. If Slater wasn't going to guard the safe, there was no other candidate except himself and he sure didn't want to spend the next day or two in this freezer. "Look, Jack. Maybe you ought to reconsider and at least stay on until we get to Santa Fe."

"I got a lady friend here," Jack confessed. "I was going to visit her a couple of days until the pass cleared. Relax and have some fun then continue on to Santa Fe."

"But you'd have to buy a ticket then, wouldn't you?"

"Yeah, but . . ."

"Tell you what," Longarm said. "If you stay on this train to Santa Fe, I'll give you ten bucks for guarding that safe and watching over these three hard cases. Ten bucks plus the money you'll save on buying your own train ticket ought to make it worth your while to stay."

Slater gave the offer serious consideration. "I'd get the ten bucks right now?"

"No. When we get to Santa Fe."

"And all I have to do is guard the safe and crack these three fellas on the skull if they get feisty? No snow shoveling if we get stuck on the pass because my bum knee won't stand up to that kind of work."

"No snow shoveling."

"Let me see the ten dollars, Marshal."

Longarm showed him the money.

"All right, then. I'll stay, but could you stop by and tell my girl friend that I had to go on to Santa Fe, but I'll be back for her when the weather clears? And tell her that I'll bring a bottle and a powerful need for lovin'."

"I'd be happy to do that if it doesn't take long."

"It won't," Slater assured him. "If she isn't working the desk downstairs, Rosie is staying upstairs in room number two at the Palace Hotel."

"Okay."

"She borrowed five dollars from me the last time I visited and you can tell her I'd like to be repaid."

"Sure," Longarm told the ex-cowboy. "Five dollars. Want me to collect for you if she has the money?"

"I'd like that fine," Slater agreed. "My mother in Santa Fe is feelin' poorly and I could use the money in case I have to haul her fat behind to a sawbones."

"All right then," Longarm said. "Rosie. Room number two at the Palace Hotel."

"That's right. Tell her Jack is sure missin' her and to save some lovin' for me next week."

"I will."

Satisfied he'd done the best he could do to hang onto his guard during the most miserable stretch of the tracks, Longarm headed into town. He'd been there before and knew that the Palace Hotel sure wasn't any palace. In fact, it was a flophouse that catered to men down on their luck and short of cash. Well, he'd promised Slater and he'd keep his promise, but not until he sent Billy Vail a telegram advising him of potential delays trying to get over Raton Pass.

The streets were slippery and choked with snow and ice. Longarm made his way up East Main Street past the old brick Victorian houses and the Spanish adobe houses, most impressive of which were the Baca House and the Bloom Mansion. He entered the business district with snow driving into his eyes and saw a mercantile. Stomping snow from his boots and wiping it off his coat, he ducked inside.

"Howdy," the proprietor said. "You sure look cold and wet."

"I am."

"A man needs a hat out in that kind of weather."

"I had one," Longarm said. "It blew off in the wind."

"Well, I got one that won't go anywhere."

The hat he showed Longarm wasn't much for style but it was long on substance. Shorter brimmed, it wouldn't catch as much air and it was part wool with ear flaps. Just the thing for this awful weather.

"How much?"

"Only five dollars."

"I'll take it," Longarm decided.

He bought some extra woolen socks and a pair of wool-lined mittens with waterproof canvas, just in case he had to help dig the train out of some snowbank. Then he found the telegraph office and it was filled with anxious railroad employees and passengers.

"Excuse me," Longarm said, stepping to the head of the line. "I'm a United States marshal and I have to send a quick telegram. It's official business."

The people in line gave him the kind of glares that told him what they thought he ought to do with his "official business" but Longarm ignored them and sent a quick telegram to Billy Vail in Denver advising him of the possible delay at Raton Pass. Just to tweak the others a tad, he grinned and said, "Thanks for your understanding and patience."

Having sent his telegram, Longarm slogged through a snowbank to a saloon where he had quick shot of whiskey to fortify himself against the elements and then purchased a bottle to take back to the train. It cost him four dollars but the bartender said it was his best brand of whiskey.

"You people really going to try and take that train over Raton Pass in this kind of weather?" the bartender asked.

"That's the plan."

"You'd be better off staying here in Trinidad until the weather clears. Get up there and you might freeze to death."

"Not with this in my hand," Longarm replied, waving the bottle. "Got any nickel cheroots?"

"Sure, how many you want?"

"Half dozen ought to hold me."

With a pocket full of cheap cigars and a ready bottle

of good whiskey and a pretty woman waiting back on the train, Longarm figured he could stand whatever misery Raton Pass had to offer.

He checked his pocket watch and saw that everything was going along quite smoothly. He still had forty-five minutes until the train departed.

"Palace Hotel. Room number two. Rosie," he reminded himself out loud.

Longarm screwed his hat down and headed for the hotel which he knew was just a couple of doors up the street. When he walked into the lobby, it was full of broke-down and busted cowboys, miners and lumbermen that reminded him of Jack Slater. They were all clustered around the big stove in the middle of the lobby and when Longarm appeared, they gave him a good going over but said nothing.

"I'm looking for Rosie," he told the hotel desk clerk, a slack-jawed fella in his sixties with eyebrows so bushy they stuck out an inch from his forehead.

"She's probably sleepin' or entertainin' someone."

"I have an important message for her."

The desk clerk had hardly glanced up at Longarm from the wrinkled newspaper he was scanning. Now, though, he gave Custis a second look and his eye fell on the bottle of whiskey. "Well, sir," he drawled, loud enough for everyone in the lobby to overhear, "you look like the kind of young fella that brings Rosie the kind of gift she most enjoys. So go on up and have a good time."

Longarm heard the snickers and it annoyed him enough to say, "I just want to tell her that . . ."

"I got no memory for messages," the clerk interrupted. "You got a message for sweet Rosie, you have to take it on up yourself."

"Fine," Longarm snorted, heading for the stairs that led up to the second floor.

When he knocked Rosie called, "Who is it?"

"Custis."

"Hold on a minute! I'm a'comin'!"

When the door swung open, Longarm's jaw dropped because he was standing face-to-face with a great big naked woman. She had a head of wild red hair and massive breasts. And while Rosie was plump, she was also damned good-looking in a rough, go-for-broke sort of way.

Rosie sized him up in a split second even to the bottle clutched in his fist. Grabbing Longarm by his coat front, she almost yanked him off his feet as she dragged him into the room and slammed the door.

"By damned," she said, propelling him backwards to sprawl across her bed. "Finally, a *real* man!"

He tried to get off the bed before she landed astraddle of him and wrestled the bottle out of his fist. Longarm yelled, "Now wait a minute, Rosie. I didn't come here to have a high old time with you."

"Oh yeah, well what *did* you come to do with me?" she demanded, yanking the cork out of the bottle with her teeth and taking a long, shuddering pull.

"I have a message from Jack Slater. He says he . . ."

"Aw, screw that cheesy little piss ant! He's got a pecker no longer nor bigger around than my little pinky! But I expect you got something that will satisfy me just fine!"

Longarm struggled to throw the heavy woman off, but the mattress was so flaccid and he was sunken down in it so deep it was like trying to crawl out of a hole. And with his big coat on and his sleeves pinned by her knees, Rosie had him in a fix.

"Have a drink before we get this party started," she said, using one hand to pry open his jaw.

Longarm gulped, whiskey running down the sides of his mouth. He managed to say, "Jack says that you owe him five dollars. He'd like it back on account of his sick mother might need to see a doctor."

Rosie passed wind and guffawed. "His sick mother has always been sick! I've known her five years. The old biddy used to live here in Trinidad. Skinny, whining old crow! World would be better off if she cashed in her chips."

Longarm could see that Rosie wasn't the sympathetic type. But she was fast with her fingers. In fact, she already had his pants open and was dragging out his rod.

"Big, but pretty flabby still," she observed, taking another swallow of whiskey and adding, "but I'll bet I can fix that damned quick!"

Before he could reply, she bent over and sucked his manhood.

"I thought you were Jack's woman."

"Not right now, I'm not!"

Longarm didn't put up much of a struggle. Rosie was an expert and had him standing up as stiff and proud as a flagpole in no time. Then the woman spread her legs and sat down on him like a huge hen on her nest crying, "Come on, Big Boy! This is gonna cost you five dollars which you can pay that skinny little turd Jack Slater. Fair enough!"

Longarm had always refused to pay a woman for pleasure but this was a unique situation. Besides that, Rosie was milking him like the world was about to end. Dragging out his pocket watch, Longarm gasped, "I only got fifteen minutes before the train pulls out."

"Big Boy, if you can stand this for *five* minutes you are gonna be the grand champion humper-thumper of Colorado!"

Longarm wasn't sure if he lasted five minutes or not. He did know that Rosie lost control first and when he shot her full of his seed, finally dislodged and sent her tumbling off the bed, he had only six minutes until the train departure.

"Leave that bottle!" she commanded.

But Longarm grabbed it and blasted through the door before Rosie could lay her hands either on him or the whiskey. Pants still unbuckled and looking for all the world like he'd just been run off by a husband or a father, Longarm lost his footing and tumbled down the stairs into the lobby which thoroughly delighted the motley crowd.

His bottle went rolling into their midst and they fell on it like wild and starved animals.

To hell with it, Longarm thought. *I've suffered enough indignity already and I'd better save my strength for the pass.*

Buckling his pants and watching the bunch of misfits begin to brawl over the whiskey, Longarm headed back out into the snowstorm. Rosie had reeked of cheap perfume. He sure hoped that the blowing snow scoured her scent away before he met up with Irene. Otherwise, the rest of his journey wasn't going to be near as pleasurable as he'd anticipated.

Chapter 6

As the train climbed out of Trinidad moving south, Longarm sat in the parlor car quietly sipping whiskey, his attention absorbed by the falling snow. He guessed they were at an elevation approaching seven thousand feet. Snow plows driven by powerful steam locomotives had already cleared the tracks many times so that they were now surrounded by a wall sometimes ten feet high. It often completely obscured the view giving him the impression that they were passing through a timeless and unworldly white tunnel.

Occasionally they would pass over a trestle or higher ground where the view opened up and then he would catch blurry images of great, snow-covered pines through the windows. Far to the west, Longarm could barely see the towering peaks of the majestic Sangre de Cristo mountains. The storm was getting worse and Longarm remembered that the summit of the pass was nearly another thousand feet higher.

"Look," he said to the woman beside him, "three big elk."

Irene had been reading a newspaper but now she

glanced up a moment before the elk vanished. "I wonder how they survive at this time of year."

"Many don't. Either they starve or grow so weak that the wolves and mountain lions pull them down."

Irene sighed. "It's true that life is utterly merciless."

Longarm placed his glass of whiskey on the table. "It's not merciless, it's *indifferent*. Life is neither fair nor unfair. It plays no favorites and it has no grudges."

"That sounds pretty fatalistic."

"It's the truth. And do you know what? I've met men who are like nature. They have no sense of good or bad. No morality. Whatever gets in their way—and by that I mean whatever opposes them—either moves aside or dies. They are people without conscience."

Irene studied his face. "Custis, please don't be offended by this question, but how much of a conscience do *you* have?"

"I think I've got as much as most men. But when I'm on the trail of a killer or a rapist or someone who has proved themselves a menace to our society, I act according to the law of the land and that of basic self-preservation."

"Like a mountain lion preying on a weakened elk."

"Exactly," Longarm agreed. "Only I'm acting as an agent of society with a sworn oath to uphold the law."

"Have you killed many men?"

He expelled a sigh of regret. "Yes, far too many."

"How many?"

"I honestly don't know. I killed soldiers in the war between the states and I've killed a good number of outlaws while being a United States marshal."

"Forgive me for asking, but do their deaths haunt you?"

Longarm emptied, then slowly refilled his glass. "Irene, these are tough but important questions. Why are you asking?"

"I'd like to know how a man like yourself feels about taking the lives of other human beings."

"Sometimes, when I've shot a man who has done something terrible . . . like killing a defenseless woman or child, I actually feel good. I feel like I've administered swift and uncompromised justice. Other times, like in the war when brave men fought each other for an ideal that most didn't completely understand, I felt very bad. There were some battles and war memories that I expect will trouble me to the grave."

"I see." She covered his hand with her own. "I hope my questions weren't too disturbing or personal."

"They were," he confessed. "But if you're wondering whether or not I'm haunted by the ghosts of Confederate soldiers, I'm not. In the war, I was under orders to kill. I had soldiers beside me whose lives depended on me holding up my end of the fight. If I'd let them down and men had died because of my negligence or cowardice, then I'd have betrayed their trust and my own self integrity. And as a federal officer of the law, I have always tried to arrest a man before taking his life."

"You didn't try to arrest those men that were mugging me back in Denver."

"I killed the first man to save myself and I shot the second after a warning. If he'd have escaped, I have no doubt that he would have mugged and perhaps murdered another innocent person. In my mind, by killing that pair, I not only saved your life and my life, but I saved other lives."

"That's an interesting way to look at it," Irene said.

"Interesting isn't the right word," Longarm told her. "It's the true way of looking at it. Those two were without conscience and they didn't care if you lived or died. In fact, they would have probably made sure that you died because then you could never have identified them."

"Will you probably have to kill men in Arizona?"

"I sure hope not. Actually, I'm going there to try and save a woman's life."

Irene's eyebrows lifted in question. "Who are you talking about?"

"Her name is Big Lips Lilly Cameron. Have you heard of her?"

"Oh yes," Irene replied. "Anyone from Arizona knows that fascinating story."

"Have you met her?"

"No, thank heavens! But I've heard plenty about Big Lips. Why do you think such a woman might be innocent?"

"I don't," Longarm answered. "But there are important people who have doubts and my job is to find out the truth."

"I've heard . . . well, never mind what I've heard. My mother said, 'If you can't say something nice about someone don't say anything at all.' I will say this . . . Lilly Cameron has a notorious reputation."

"Just as I'm sure I do among the acquaintances of men I've either killed or sent to a judge's death sentence."

Irene leaned her head on Longarm's shoulder. "Do you mind if I offer you a suggestion?"

"No."

"I think you should quit your job and settle into something with a more promising future. You could do many things very well."

"You don't know that."

"Sure I do," Irene argued. "There are plenty of things that a brave man of action is well suited for besides administering the long arm of the law. In fact, you might even consider studying the law and some day becoming a judge."

Longarm scoffed at the idea. "That could never be my cup of tea."

"Why not?"

"Because I couldn't stand to see the guilty set free to commit the same crimes again and again due to lack of evidence. I'd be so frustrated by the confines of the law that I'd resign."

"You could start a profitable business and become financially successful."

"What kind of business?"

Irene shrugged. "I don't know. Gunsmithing?"

"No thanks."

"Freighting?"

"I hate mules."

"What about becoming a rancher?"

He laughed. "In the first place, I have no money to buy a ranch that would support me and a herd of cattle. In the second place, the only interest I have in a cow is if it's hot and on my supper plate."

"You're impossible."

"Maybe so," he admitted. "But. . . ."

Longarm's words were cut short by the locomotive's piercing wail and then the screech of wheels grinding against cold, icy iron rails. The train was sliding to a stop and then it hit something that knocked everyone forward.

"We struck something big," Longarm said.

"What could it possibly be?"

"A tree toppled by the weight of snow on its branches or maybe a huge boulder that broke loose and rolled down on the tracks. And worst of all, there might have been an avalanche."

"Oh my gosh! I hadn't thought of that possibility. If it's an avalanche, what could we do?"

"Depends on its size," Longarm told her. "If not too much snow is covering the tracks, we'll probably be asked to dig it out. But if it's wide and deep, we'll have no choice but to reverse power and return to Trinidad."

"I sure hope that's not the case."

"Me too. But for the moment we might as well sit here

53

and relax. Pretty quick the conductor will tell us what happened and needs to be done."

Irene kissed his cheek. "You are so practical. So . . . unflappable."

"It helps in my line of work."

"Would we have time to go to my compartment and knock one off?"

"Good idea," he said, grinning from ear to ear.

"Oh," she added as they started to rise from their seats. "One thing and I hope you won't take it wrong."

"What's that?"

"Well, whatever that new cologne is that you bought in Trinidad, I wish you'd stop using it until we have to part company. I know that you have good intentions, but the stuff almost gags me."

Longarm turned away so that she couldn't read the expression on his face then he mumbled, "I'll wash it off and use it no more."

"Thank you."

As Longarm predicted, the conductor soon appeared. He looked upset when he announced, "I'm afraid that we've stuck a boulder that was hurled down in an avalanche. The track is closed and it's going to take some time to learn if there is any chance of getting through the snow or if we have to return to Trinidad."

A gambler who had been sitting at a table nearby protested, "Dammit! I have to get to Santa Fe by tomorrow."

"I'm afraid that it's too early to tell yet what we should do next."

"Well we can't go back!" the gambler snapped. "A delay could cost me hundreds of dollars."

Longarm decided that he didn't care for the man's manner or looks. The gambler was thin, unshaven and dirty with shifty eyes and long, delicate fingers.

"Mister," Longarm said, "we've all got business to take

care of down the line. But complaining isn't going to help."

The gambler had been drinking heavily and it gave him courage. "The conversation was between myself and the conductor, so you should mind your own damned business."

Longarm jumped out of his seat. It took him only a moment to reach the gambler and sink his fingertips into the man's thin shoulder. "You're talking to a United States marshal and you need to keep your mouth shut. Furthermore, if we have to dig through a field of snow, you're going to be expected to help."

The gambler squirmed with pain. "My health wouldn't permit shoveling snow! You're hurting me!"

Longarm snatched the man's bottle from his grasp and handed it to the conductor. "This fella needs to sober up and behave himself. No more whiskey for him."

The gambler's dark eyes flashed with outrage. "You have no right to take that bottle. You're. . . ."

Longarm's fingers again bit into the man's shoulder, but harder this time, causing his already pale face to turn ghostly white. He cried, "Stop it! I can't stand pain!"

Releasing the gambler, Longarm stepped back saying, "You sober up and get ready to work. We're all in this together and I won't stand for any slackers among the men. Is that understood?"

The gambler managed to nod his head.

Longarm returned to Irene who leaned close and whispered, "Weren't you a little hard on him?"

"His kind doesn't appreciate subtlety."

The train sat for almost an hour before one of the engineers appeared covered with snow and shivering from the cold. "Ladies and gentlemen," he announced, "the track is covered with about six feet of snow for a distance of fifty yards. We can ram our way through part of it but the impact puts us in danger of creating an even bigger and more destructive avalanche."

"Then we can't do that," someone said.

"You're right," the engineer agreed. "It would be extremely unwise. But there is one other alternative and that is simply to reverse our direction and back down this mountain into Trinidad."

"The hell with that!" the gambler yelled. "We paid this railroad to deliver us to Santa Fe and that's what you're going to do!"

Longarm twisted around in his seat and his hard glare was enough to prevent any further outbursts from the man. Addressing the engineer he asked, "Would our lives be in danger if we got out and started to dig our way forward?"

"Of course," the engineer replied. "However, I believe the risk would be small. But you have to remember that there is also a risk in backing all the way down this mountain to Trinidad. We've already passed several of the most dangerous stretches for avalanches and there's no guarantee that our retreat has not already been completely blocked."

Longarm nodded with understanding.

The engineer looked past him to the other dozen or so passengers in the car and said, "Folks, every one of you was advised earlier that there was a risk to board the train in the hope that we could get over Raton Pass without serious difficulty."

"So what do you recommend?" a heavyset woman demanded.

"My recommendation is that every man on board follow me into the mail car where we have a large number of snow shovels and tools. I think we can dig our way through this patch of snow in a few hours and be over the mountain before dark. But it will take a great effort

56

on all our parts and even then there is no guarantee of success."

"That's what we'll do," Longarm decided. "Every man on board will pitch in and we'll do our best to be in Raton before darkness sets in and the cold deepens."

"But there's a blizzard out there!" the gambler protested, looking around at his fellow passengers as if they were all insane. "Don't you people realize that you can get frostbite or pneumonia in that kind of weather? Or that you could simply freeze and die?"

"No one is going to get frostbite or pneumonia and they aren't going to die," Longarm said, irked by the gambler's mounting hysteria. "The women can keep the potbellied stoves on board fired up and hot cups of coffee coming to those outside. We can take turns manning the shovels and work in short shifts so that no one gets too cold or works to the point of exhaustion."

The gambler wasn't buying that. "So, Marshal, now you're a doctor and you're going to know exactly when each one of us is on the verge of freezing or sickness?"

Longarm wanted to deck the gambler, but instead curbed the urge and said, "Everyone get your heaviest coats and gloves, then come to the mail car without delay. We don't have time to waste arguing."

The gambler tried to hang back but Longarm propelled the man out of his chair and down the aisle warning, "Get your coat on and get a shovel or I'll toss you out just as you are right now."

They made their way past the sleeping compartments and second-class to the mail car, and when they opened the door the engineer jumped back with a loud cry of alarm.

"What's the matter?" Longarm shouted, bulling his way forward.

"He's . . . he's dead!"

Longarm pulled up short and stared down at Jack Slater's body which was lying in a cold pool of already congealing blood. No one had to tell Custis that Jack's throat had been cut from ear to ear. And the reason for the murder was obvious. The three toughs that Longarm had pistol-whipped and laid out on the floor were gone . . . and so was the gold and cash that had been in the safe because the chain that had held the door shut had been sawed in half.

"What's wrong up there!" a small man behind Longarm asked. "Why are we. . . ."

Longarm turned to see the man's expression and it wasn't pretty as he gasped, "Oh my God!"

Finding a blanket, Longarm covered Slater's face, torso and as much of the congealing pool of blood as possible. Then he said to the horrified passengers who had already appeared, "There are three killers out there trying to escape with the contents of that safe."

"They'll never make it to either Trinidad or Raton," the engineer whispered. "They'll freeze first, and I for one couldn't be happier."

"Probably so, but they must have thought they had a chance or they wouldn't have killed Slater and gone to all the work of sawing that chain. So I guess I'm going to have to make sure."

"You mean. . . ."

"I mean I have to make sure they don't survive," Longarm said, his voice hard and flat. "So you'll be in charge of the digging and I'll go after those three."

"But their tracks will be wiped out by the blowing snow."

"Not yet."

The engineer shook his head. "Marshal, even if you did find them alive, how would you get them back here in a blizzard?"

Longarm wasn't prepared to answer that question. And even though he was a lawman, he wasn't sure he wanted to risk freezing in order to save poor Jack Slater's cold-blooded killers.

Chapter 7

"By the way," Longarm asked the conductor, "does anyone know how much gold and cash were in that old safe?"

"Sure someone knows, but they're either in Denver or San Francisco. Does it matter?"

"It might," Longarm told the man. "If the gold was in the form of heavy bars, then it ought to slow the thieves down."

"It wasn't in bars," the conductor said. "I saw the guards load it on board and I'd guess it couldn't have weighed more than fifty pounds. Probably gold dust or nuggets. The rest was all cash."

"Fifty pounds is a lot of weight to carry though deep snow," Longarm said. "Did you or any of the engineers happen to see which direction they headed?"

"They headed straight down this mountain," the conductor told him. "You won't have any trouble picking up their tracks but, given this damned falling snow, I wouldn't expect they'd hold up but a few more hours."

"That might be all I need. Tell Miss Hanson not to worry and that I'll be back."

"I'll tell her. You be careful, Marshal. If you don't catch up with 'em in an hour or two, you should give it up and come back to the train. Otherwise, we might pull out. Once this track is cleared, we can't risk the danger of waiting for you."

"I know that. And I wouldn't expect you to wait for me. Just don't let that gambler get out of pulling his fair share of the work load."

"I won't."

Longarm drew his hat down tight and turned up the collar on his coat muttering, "I sure hope this storm passes before long."

"So do we. Be careful, Marshal. There isn't much shelter up in these mountains. Just a few old cabins built by the first trappers and mountain men to pass through this country hunting for beaver."

"I could use a rifle."

"I'll get you one. Hold on a minute."

While the conductor hurried off to get a rifle, Longarm watched the passengers unload from the train with their snow shovels. They were a grim lot and, except for the Italian and his son, most of them didn't look like they were capable of doing a great deal of work. Still, they had to realize that their lives were in jeopardy and their fates very much in their own hands. Sure, there was coal on board and probably enough food to last for a week, but if they were snow-bound for that long, they'd all suffer.

"Here you go," the conductor said. "It's my own Winchester. The locomotive engineer keeps it up front to warn off cattle and train robbers."

Longarm inspected the weapon. It was loaded and although the stock was battered and scarred, the rifle appeared in good working order. "How's it shoot?"

"Just a tad high at fifty yards. By that, I mean at that distance you'd aim at a man's crotch if you wanted to drill him in the heart."

"That's good to know."

"And here's some extra cartridges. I hope you find those three men frozen to death but, if you don't, I wouldn't try to capture and bring them back alive. Too dangerous."

Longarm nodded but knew he couldn't execute anyone. The conversation he'd shared with Irene about death and morality had given him much to think about and he still hadn't come up with any easy answers. He thought he could live with the men he'd killed but knew they might catch up with him someday.

One of the passengers held back from the others and it was difficult to see who the man was, but Longarm figured it had to be the gambler. He took a step in that man's direction, changed his mind and headed on down the mountain at an angle until he came upon the tracks left by the three killer-thieves. The tracks were deep and Longarm felt sure that they would not disappear for the rest of the day.

I'll catch them within an hour, he thought. *And either they'll surrender peacefully and carry the loot back to the train, or I'll gun them down with no more mercy than they had when they slit Jack Slater's throat.*

Longarm had underestimated the strength and condition of the three men. In retrospect, he realized that had been foolish because they had been hard men well accustomed to the altitude and outdoors. Probably more accustomed to it than he was. Still, they were carrying gold and breaking the trail through the deep snow drifts while all he had to do was to follow. So Longarm knew that he was overtaking them but it was going to take longer than expected.

At least the storm seemed to be passing. There was snow still flying but most of it was being whipped off the trees by the icy wind. Longarm's underclothes were clammy with perspiration and he was thankful that the men he was chasing had gone down the mountain instead of in the opposite direction. Even so, his breath came in short, fast bursts and it was hard to keep his footing on the packed snow and ice.

Out of the corner of his eye, Longarm caught a glimpse of a brown, flashing blur. His rifle came up but he didn't fire as a four-pronged white tailed deer struggled through the trees. It had been coming toward him but veered sharply to his left. Longarm crouched in the deep snow, breathing quick clouds of steam because of his exertion. He was sweating and short of breath but all his senses were fixed ahead. Something had startled that buck and caused it to break from its shelter and that something was probably the men he sought.

They're very close now, he told himself. *Probably not more than a few hundred yards ahead.*

Without deep snow, he'd have made every effort to quickly overtake the men, possibly even to circle around and lie in wait. But with the snow and extreme cold he knew that it would be foolish to overexert himself. Longarm was already perspiring heavily under his wool-lined leather jacket and unless he slowed his heart beat he was going to have trouble making an accurate shot at any distance.

"Just settle down, Custis," he warned himself. "Take this last part slow and easy. Let them be the ones that are shiverin' and shakin' and out of breath. You be the one that is steady."

Longarm took his own advice very seriously. More times than he cared to admit, Longarm's quarry had panicked and shot wildly or did something foolish resulting in their own death. In the heat of a life-or-death struggle between adversaries, far better to be the one in complete control.

So Longarm dropped down on his knees so that his head couldn't even be seen above the snow line and then waited until his breath slowed and his heart quit pounding. Then he slowly raised to his full height and moved forward placing each foot in the killers' tracks.

The outlaws' trail entered a patch of thick pines and Longarm was extra careful as he crept along, all his senses heightened. He stopped often and listened until he heard their faint and indistinct voices. They were still too far ahead for Longarm to understand what they were saying but he could tell that they were miserable and unhappy. Probably arguing.

After a short distance, the tracks emerged from the stand of timber and entered a long meadow. That's when Longarm saw the three men and he was surprised that they were less than seventy-five yards ahead. Dropping to his knees, he raised his head just high enough to witness their struggle through the deep snow. They were headed back into another stand of pines but keeping to a straight line down the mountainside. The snow had quit falling and the temperature, if anything, seemed to drop until the very air was frozen. Longarm's face was numb and his eyes wept.

If you call for them to surrender now, they could get into the trees, he thought. *Better wait until you can catch them with more open space around them so they can't break for cover.*

Waiting was always a hard thing to do and never more so than now in this bitter temperature. Still, Longarm didn't relish the idea of going into heavy forest after three experienced woodsmen. So he allowed his quarry to enter the forest again and he stayed back far enough that there was no possibility they could overhear his approach.

This time the stand of pines continued for more than a mile and Longarm had to keep stopping or he would have overtaken the three killers who were obviously having an increasingly difficult time breaking trail. Most likely, that was because they were also nearing the point of exhaustion and the deepening cold was taking its toll even on their hard bodies.

Finally, just when Longarm's patience was nearly depleted, the trees opened onto another meadow. One of the killers whooped with joy and that was when Longarm saw the log cabin.

"So all the time they knew exactly where they were going," he whispered. "And if they reach that cabin they could hold me off until I freeze to death."

There was no choice for Longarm but to make his stand right now, even though the firing distance between himself and the killers was greater than he would have liked.

Longarm removed his gloves. Levering a shell into the breech of the Winchester, he put the rifle to his shoulder. Taking aim on the lead man's crotch, he shouted, "United States marshal. Freeze!"

The three men spun around in unison and when they fumbled under their coats for their weapons, Longarm had no choice and opened fire. His first shot missed because the rifle shot high. Lowering his aim to the level of the man's knees, he fired a second round and his bullet caught the killer in his stomach. The man bent over howling like a dying dog and now that Longarm had the rifle sighted, he drilled the second killer in the side. The man fell and then jumped up and ran after the third train robber who hadn't made the mistake of trying to match a pistol against a Winchester.

Longarm shot the one nearing the cabin between his shoulder blades. His target went down on a patch of ice, body skidding into a snow drift. But the last outlaw raced past his fallen companion and despite Longarm's bullets made it into the cabin. He might have taken another bullet as he tore open the door and threw himself inside.

"Dammit!" Longarm swore, breaking into as much of a run as the snow would allow.

He was still about fifty yards from the cabin when the man inside showed half of his body from behind the door and opened fire with his revolver. Longarm dove into the snow but not before he felt a bullet whistle past his ear and then another clip his scalp, causing him drop the rifle and momentarily lose consciousness.

If the last of the train robbers had been able or willing, he might have seized his advantage and killed Longarm while he was helpless. But the outlaw was wounded and so the best that he could do was to stumble out of the cabin and fire until he ran out of bullets. Cursing and screaming, he tore off his coat trying to reach the extra cartridges stuffed into the loops of his gun belt. His bare, nearly frozen fingers dropped bullets into the snow as he advanced.

Dimly, Longarm heard the man's curses. He tore at the buttons of his own coat and when he finally got it open, the handle of his Colt had the feel of an icicle. Drawing it from his holster, Longarm shoved the weapon forward through the snow. The killer was almost on top of him when they both opened fire.

Longarm felt another bullet strike him somewhere, and then everything went black and cold, and he again lost consciousness.

Chapter 8

Longarm awoke hearing the raucous, incessant caw-caw of a raven. The huge bird was standing in the snow only a couple of dozen yards from where he lay and it was upset. What Longarm wanted to do was close his eyes and go back to sleep, but the raven was creating such a ruckus that sleep was impossible. Pushing himself up on his elbows, Longarm stared at the bird and then looked down to see that a small patch of snow under his side was colored crimson. But at least it had quit snowing.

Remembering he had been shot, Longarm twisted around to see a dead man staring at him through frosted eyes. The raven demanded his attention so he turned back to it and frowned.

"What's your problem? Do you want to pick my friend's eyes out, but you're worried because I'm still half alive?"

The bird cocked its head to one side and squawked with defiance.

"Raven, you can have his eyes for all I care," Longarm said, retrieving his borrowed Winchester, "because your loud mouth might just have saved my life."

Longarm pushed himself into a sitting position. It was

no longer snowing but the coldness had intensified. He realized that he had been grazed across the ribs and the snow had effectively stanched the bleeding.

Get up and get into the cabin before you freeze to death, he told himself. *It will be dark soon.*

With the huge black raven still giving him a piece of its mind, Longarm struggled to his feet. He took two clumsy steps and the world began to spin so fast that he collapsed but did not quite lose consciousness. Realizing that if he did lose consciousness he might never awaken, Longarm decided to grab his Winchester and crawl to the cabin.

The raven hopped along beside him but kept well out of arm's reach. With the bird's cries goading him forward, it took Longarm only a few minutes to reach the cabin and then to drag himself to its rough stone fireplace. The raven remained outside but it sounded angrier than ever at being left in the cold.

The cabin was every bit as frigid as the outside world. Still, as his benumbed mind surveyed his new surroundings, Longarm realized the cabin contained a stack of firewood and several wooden boxes of what he hoped were food and supplies. That made sense, considering the train robbers must have intended to come here after breaking open the safe. In fact, it was entirely possible that a fourth member of the gang had created the avalanche that had covered the tracks. Given the steep terrain and deep snows, starting an avalanche wouldn't have been difficult. Just a few shots or maybe the detonation of a stick of dynamite.

But, if there was a fourth member of the gang . . . where was he now? And where was the gold and cash taken from the train's safe?

Longarm had not thought of searching the bodies, but he hadn't seen any sign of the robbers carrying heavy bags of gold. Still, fifty pounds divided three ways was not much weight and could have been stuffed in their coat pockets. Longarm wanted to go outside and search the bodies, but he decided that would have to wait until morning. Right now, he was just too weak and exhausted to go back out into the failing light and freezing cold.

Longarm's wound now throbbed with pain. He needed to get a fire started. After that, he could warm up and look for some food to cook. Later, he'd give some thought to the gold and cash.

Longarm had difficulty getting his fire started. His hands were shaking so badly that he kept breaking matches and when one did flare, it was snuffed out by the wind blasting through the open door. So he shut the door, then managed to start his fire. Soon the tiny cabin began to warm, but the chimney was so small that it didn't vent all of the wood smoke.

Coughing and feeling dizzy, Longarm partially re-opened the door to help clear the room of the noxious smoke. The raven was still outside squawking, but he ignored the noisy bird and studied the large open meadow that he and the three dead fugitives had crossed. He was looking to see if there was a fourth train robber on his way to the cabin.

Seeing no one, but growing increasingly convinced that he would soon have an unwelcome visitor, Longarm decided he had better inspect the interior of the cabin to see what provisions had been stocked. He soon uncovered a box of tinned food in addition to a smoked ham, sacks of flour, beans and potatoes as well as several pounds of well-seasoned jerked beef. Even more of a find were two bottles of whiskey and a box of decent cigars.

"Thank you, thank you," he muttered to himself as he found a glass and poured a drink. Then he tossed the whiskey down, lit a cigar and knew he was well on the road to recovery.

His meal was ready by the time his cigar was a stub,

so Longarm ate well and then he opened the cabin door a crack. The cold snaked through the doorway and he shut it tight again. No, he would keep to his plan and wait until morning to inspect the bodies of the dead men. If he found the stolen money and gold, then he could rest assured that the three men had acted on their own without the help of a fourth member. Perhaps they had fully intended to end up here, and hide out for a week or two until any search parties gave up, and then drift down into Raton or back to Trinidad, putting even more miles behind them before they fully enjoyed their plunder.

However, if the three men were *not* carrying the stolen loot, then it seemed pretty obvious that there had been a fourth and maybe even more partners. In that case, Longarm knew that his life was still in grave danger. In his favor was the fact that the storm had dumped a tremendous amount of snow and anyone trying to reach this cabin would have a real physical challenge. The downside was that he had no intention of holing up here any longer than it took him to regain his strength and head for the nearest town or settlement.

There were blankets in the cabin so Longarm spread them out in front of the fireplace, tried to dampen the fire so that most of the smoke would make it up the chimney, and then he fell asleep with his gun close at hand.

He slept well and when he awoke he initially thought it was still night. However, when he consulted his pocket watch by the light of the dying fire, he saw that it was half past eight o'clock in the morning. Longarm got up and went to the door. When he pried it open, it was snowing again and wolves had been at work on the three dead train robbers.

Longarm pulled on his coat and gloves, then his boots which had been drying by the fire.

He bulled his way through the deep snow to the nearest

body which wasn't a pretty sight, given that the wolves had devoured the man's extremities. Checking the victim's coat pockets, Longarm found neither cash nor gold. The same was true of the other two men. That meant that there had been at least one other member of this gang on board the train who had stashed the loot while these three loggers had acted as decoys to lure away any pursuers.

Longarm certainly did not owe these killers and thieves any respect, but he couldn't abide the idea of leaving them to be eaten by a pack of hungry wolves. So, one by one, he went to the trouble of dragging their bodies to the back side of the cabin. He wasn't going to have them inside thawing, but at least he could hear the wolves and drive them off if they returned. The loggers' bodies were already frozen and he stacked them up like a cord of wood against the cabin and then covered them with tree limbs. Given the falling snow, they'd soon be hidden from sight.

He felt dizzy and weak by the time he finished that unpleasant task and went back into the cabin where he ate, stoked up the fire and laid down to rest after having bolted the door.

Longarm slept well into the afternoon and awakened feeling refreshed and clearheaded. He melted snow and used it to boil potatoes and beef, then ate a prodigious meal.

Now he had a decision to make. Either he could wait out the storm, maybe even getting lucky enough to have other members of the train robbery appear, or he could leave the cabin and brave the elements hoping to find a road that would lead him to a timber camp or a mountain settlement.

It wasn't an easy decision. If it hadn't been for his being badly needed in Williams, Arizona, to investigate the murder charges against Big Lips Lilly Cameron, Longarm would have hunkered down and waited out the storm. But time was of the essence, so he rebandaged and

71

wrapped his side wound and fashioned a sled out of the wooden boxes that he would use to drag along food and supplies. Under a rotting bear skin piled in the corner of the cabin he found a pair of ancient snowshoes. Unfortunately, they needed considerable repair work and that also took him a few hours.

Longarm wasn't sure if he should hike back up the mountain and try to intercept the next train at Raton Pass or if he should take the easier way and go downhill and hope to find help. After careful deliberation, he decided to hike back up the mountain until he reached the train tracks. They might well be covered but he'd be able to see where the railroad had sliced through the hills, and he could follow those tracks over the pass and down to Raton.

He spent one more night resting and feasting, trying to regain every last bit of his strength for the hard climb and weather he would face just to reach the tracks. Then he caught a break when the storm passed and the next morning turned sunny and warm enough to begin melting the deep snow.

"Luck is finally with me," he told the raven, which still lingered around the cabin.

Longarm felt good and he paced himself up the mountainside. The snowshoes were cumbersome but indispensable, and the grocery box bumped along behind him just fine. It carried enough food to last three days, and, if necessary, it would also serve as kindling.

After a full day of brutal uphill work, he arrived at the tracks near sundown. Longarm was exhausted and cold, but he cleared a spot in the snow right in the middle of the tracks and made a big campfire. If the passenger train or a locomotive with a snow plow came along, they'd see his fire and stop, even in the dead of the night.

Longarm ate well and curled up near his fire, feeling he was doing the best he could given these hard circumstances. That night, he slept without dreams and when he awoke the following morning, he was gratified to find that the sky was still blue, although the air was very cold.

How much farther over the pass to Raton? he asked himself. *Seems to me that it can't be more than ten or fifteen miles. I'll bet that I'm almost at the summit, and, if I keep moving, I'll start on the down slope by this afternoon.*

Longarm melted snow and boiled more beef. He was cold to the bone, so he washed his meal down with a few gulps of whiskey, then lit a cigar and studied the snow-covered forest. Even in these dire circumstances, he could appreciate the silence and the mountain's beauty. In the springtime, this country would bloom with wildflowers of every color and the deer would venture out into the open meadows, thin but alive.

As summer progressed, the mountains would warm and be filled with sweet fragrances from the pines, flowers and grasses. It would be a fine spectacle with frequent afternoon showers and great white clouds tap-dancing their way across the highest peaks. Tall and powerful bull elk would call out their shrill, haunting challenges as they sought their mates and insured their bloodlines.

In autumn, the gold and red aspen would emblazon the draws and the deep valleys between the ridges and bear would begin to think of hibernation. The first snow would fall perhaps as early as the final weeks of September. Then, the life that inhabited these high mountains would draw into itself and prepare for the test of a long winter survival.

Longarm loved mountains more than the plains or the desert. And, had not the snow been so deep and the climb up Raton Pass through the snow so difficult, he would have enjoyed hiking in complete solitude while watching for wildlife. But the real facts he now faced were that Jack Slater had been murdered, forcing Longarm to exact his own deadly retribution. And even more troubling was that the gold and cash were missing and that meant there was at least one other killer . . . and that man was probably the mastermind.

As Longarm struggled, following the deep gully of snow where earlier trains and snowplows had passed, he wondered who among the other passengers or railroad employees could be that mastermind. One of the engineers or conductors? That was entirely possible. One of the other passengers? Why not?

Longarm wasn't sure who he was after now, except that that man had been aboard the train he'd been riding. His only hope of finding the accomplice or accomplices was to reach Raton and then to inform the proper railroad officials of his suspicions. Afterward, he would use whatever means he had at his disposal to reach Arizona and then to investigate the case that he had been assigned by Billy Vail back in Denver.

It was about noon when Longarm realized he had finally gained the summit of Raton Pass. There was a light wind blowing from the north and, although it was at his back, it blew snow off the branches of the pines to dust his hat and coat. To celebrate the completion of his long, difficult ascent of the summit, he drank a cup of whiskey and stuffed another cigar between his teeth. Chewing rather than smoking the cigar, he tightened his bindings on the old snowshoes and stared down toward New Mexico, wondering if he'd have to slog through the snow all the way to Raton or if he'd meet a train. He decided it was about seven or eight miles down to the little ranching and railroad town.

Longarm didn't have to wonder for long. In the distance, he could hear a powerful locomotive slamming its way over the pass he'd just crossed. Longarm stepped off the tracks, untied his snowshoes and lit the unchewed por-

tion of his cigar. He waited nearly an hour for the locomotive—pushing a massive snow plow and pulling only
two cars—to appear.

"Hello there!" he shouted up at the amazed engineer.
"How about a lift down to Raton!"

Over the loud huff-huffing of the steam locomotive,
Longarm saw the engineer yell down at him. When he
indicated that he couldn't hear, the man waved him to
jump on board.

Once in the cab with the engineer and the fireman,
Longarm quickly explained the reason for his being
stranded.

"Marshal," the engineer shouted, "we heard about you
taking off after them killers and was hoping you'd show
up sooner or later! You might want to go back and thaw
out in the second car."

"I'm doing just fine here beside the furnace!"

"Suit yourself."

For another three hours, Longarm sat perched in the
tiny cab of the locomotive as it battered and rammed its
way down the mountain using the massive snowplow to
clear the tracks all the way into Raton. When they finally
arrived at that little railroad and ranching community,
Longarm thanked the engineer and headed off to make
his reports.

His first stop was the telegraph office where he sent a
message explaining his situation to Billy Vail. His next
stop was the local marshal's office where lawman Abe
Packard listened with interest and kept his stove burning
hot. Longarm finished his report by saying that he had
found no gold or cash on the three men he'd shot up in
the mountains.

Marshal Packard was a small, bandy-legged former
cowboy with a habit of getting right to the point. "Marshal
Long, isn't it possible the three men you killed stashed
their loot before they reached the cabin?"

"I don't think so," Longarm replied. "In the first place, the snow was so deep that they would have had to dig a long way down just to reach the frozen ground. And, in the second place, they weren't expecting to be overtaken. I'm quite sure of that because they never once looked back or made any attempt to ambush me when I was on their trail. No, Packard, I am convinced that they never had the gold and cash that came out of that train safe."

"There was a considerable amount of cash, but only four sacks of gold," the local marshal said. "I know that because the information came to me from the railroad and security people over the wire."

"How much cash?"

"I was told in confidence that the safe contained more than thirty thousand dollars but it was all in new one hundred dollar bills."

Longarm frowned. "So one of the train's employees or a passenger could have easily hid the gold and cash either in a valise or in their suitcase."

"That's right," Packard agreed. "And, if I'd have known what you just told me about the loot not being with those three logging men, then I'd have certainly conducted a thorough search of everyone on that train."

"But you *didn't* know," Longarm said, "so it's not your fault. Are some of the passengers and employees still in Raton?"

"I would imagine so."

"Then we ought to have a talk with them right away," Longarm decided.

"You've had quite an ordeal," Packard said. "And I notice you're favoring your right side. We don't have a doctor in town but I am pretty good at fixin' gunshot wounds, bites and broken bones. Are you wounded?"

"It's nothing," Longarm answered, not wanting to lose

any more time. "The sooner we interview everyone who got off that train I was on, the better."

"I agree." Marshal Abe Packard came to his feet and reached for his heavy coat. "Let's start off by going down to the railroad office. They'll know which of their employees are still here in Raton. They might also be able to tell us which of the passengers continued on and which got off to stay here in town."

Longarm nodded in agreement. He propped his old snowshoes up against the wall near the stove prompting Packard to say, "I haven't seen a pair like that since I was a kid. Those were probably made by some old fur trapper fifty or sixty years ago. I'd like to have an old-time pair like that myself. My father was one of the first trappers in this country and he had a very similar pair."

"Then take them," Longarm said starting for the door. "They've served me well and I don't intend to have any further use for them."

Packard had two gold teeth in front, and now they flashed with pleasure. "Thank you! They'll look good on my cabin's wall over the fireplace. And by the way, it was mighty lucky you had a rifle with you out there when you had your showdown with those three buzzards."

"It's not my rifle. A conductor loaned it to me and, if he's still in Raton, I'd better find him and return that Winchester."

"What was his name?"

Longarm confessed he didn't know the man's name, but when he described him the marshal said, "That's old Ike Berry. I know where he lives."

"Good," Longarm said, eager to begin the questioning. He knew that many, if not most of the passengers that he'd started out with from Denver, would have continued on their journey and would be unavailable for questioning. That would include people like that immigrant family from Italy as well as his former traveling companion, Mrs. Irene Hanson.

Not that either the Italians or Mrs. Hanson could possibly have had anything to do with the murder of poor Jack Slater and the train robbery.

Chapter 9

Longarm and Marshal Packard's first stop was at the railroad offices. When they met the supervisor whose name was Bill Olander, the man said, "Marshal Long, we've all been mighty worried about you being alone in that blizzard up at the pass. It's a big relief to know that you've not only survived but you also administered justice to those who stole the cash and gold from our mail car."

"I wish that I could have recovered the lost gold and cash."

Olander's jaw sagged. "You mean you didn't?"

"That's right. I chased them maybe five or six miles down the mountain to an old trapper's cabin. I ordered them to halt and surrender but they chose to fight to the death and that's what they got."

"But the . . ."

"The gold and cash wasn't with them," Longarm said. "And furthermore, they didn't stop to hide it, so that only leaves one conclusion . . . they must have given the loot to someone on that train that continued on to this town."

"Are you sure?"

"Either that," Longarm said, "or they stuffed it in a snowbank."

"That would be nearly as bad," Olander said. "I mean, you rode the locomotive pushing that big plow down here and saw the huge amount of fresh snow that it pushes aside in order to open up the track. If they stuffed their loot in a snowbank it might now be buried twenty feet deep! My gosh, the money would be destroyed by the time the snow melts next spring and. . . ."

"I think that the thieves knew that there would be snow-plows working the pass," Longarm interrupted. "And I don't believe they would have left anything to chance. That's why I'm nearly certain that the cash and gold were brought here to Raton either by one of your employees or one of the passengers."

Olander surveyed his office. There were five other rail-road employees besides himself and they were all ears. "Gentlemen," he said, "we need to talk in *private*."

They went into Olander's office and shut the door. The railroad supervisor took a seat behind his desk, steepled his fingers and said, "I can't believe that any of my people would be in on something that resulted in murder."

"It wouldn't be the first time that it has happened," Longarm said, "nor the last. I understand that the loss amounted to thirty thousand dollars in one hundred dollar bills plus the bags of gold. What were they valued at?"

"Four thousand dollars," Olander said without hesitation. "Each bag held one thousand dollars' worth of gold dust."

"So that means the loss totaled thirty-four thousand," Longarm said. "Even split four or five ways, the amount is considerable."

"Yes, it is," Olander agreed. "But my people are all absolutely honest."

"We hope that's the case," Longarm told the man. "But we need to interview every one of them that was on that train. Are they all still here in Raton?"

"As a matter of fact, they are."

"Would you please give us a private room to interrogate each one and ask them to cooperate fully?" Marshal Packard asked. "I doubt that we'll take much of their time unless their answers sound fishy."

"Of course."

"We also need to know the names of the passengers."

"I don't have that information," Olander said.

Longarm frowned with disappointment. "Do you know how many of them stayed here in Raton?"

"Only four," Olander answered. "And I know them all quite well. None of them could have possibly been involved in robbery and murder."

"Write their names down for us anyway."

The railroad supervisor wrote down the names and handed them to the town marshal who said, "Bill, you know as well as I do that these are all good, upstanding citizens."

"We need to question them anyway," Longarm said. "I have to be in Arizona on a matter of life and death, so I won't be able to stay any longer than the next passenger train heading west."

"That would be tomorrow," Olander said quickly and with a relief that he didn't even bother to hide. "Unless we are hit with another blizzard and delay."

"Fine." Longarm stood up. "Let's go see those four private citizens and then we'll return here to interview the employees who were on the train when it was robbed and Mr. Slater was murdered."

"I'll have them here waiting," Olander promised. "But I swear to you that none would ever have committed such a crime. They're all outstanding employees."

"I'm sure they are," Longarm said. "But even outstanding people have been known to be corrupted by quick, easy money."

"Perhaps," the man agreed. "But not when it involves murder."

81

Longarm had put some thought to that very issue. "It's entirely possible," he said, "that whoever masterminded and set this up after recruiting the three loggers had no idea that the theft of that mail coach safe would include murdering its guard. I'd already had trouble with the loggers who were in your second-class coach. They were crude, foul-mouthed men who were harassing other passengers so bad that I had to pistol-whip them."

"I didn't know that," Marshal Packard said.

"I forgot to mention it," Longarm told the lawman. "But the point is, those three were half drunk and belligerent, in addition to suffering from my parting their scalps with my Colt revolver. Given all that, it's easy enough to see why they might have gone over the edge and killed Jack Slater, instead of simply knocking him out and tying him up while they broke into the safe by cutting those chains."

Both men nodded with understanding. A few moments later, when Longarm and Packard left the private office, every man and woman in the outer office stared at them. Exiting on the street and marching through the snow and slush ground up by many horses and wagons, Longarm drawled, "The word is out. Those people know what we're after and, if the killer is on the railroad's payroll, he'll be all that much harder to trap."

"I'm not much good at interrogating suspects," Marshal Packard admitted. "So I'll just sort of let you do it."

"That'll be fine," Longarm told the man. "But, if you hear anything that sounds wrong, be sure and let it me know."

"I will."

They spent the next two hours interviewing the four private citizens who had been on the train. One was an elderly woman who was rather flattered when she realized she was even remotely being considered a murder suspect.

"Good heavens! I'm eighty-six years old and there are

days when I can barely remember my name!" she exclaimed. "So how on earth would I have masterminded a *train* robbery?"

"I guess you couldn't have," Longarm said, feeling more than a bit foolish. "Sorry to have bothered you."

"No bother at all," she said. "In fact, this is all very thrilling. Marshal Packard, would you please let me in on it if you figure out who really planned the train robbery?"

"I sure will," he promised.

The second and third interviews were also fruitless, one being a minister and the other being a wealthy timber mill owner who would not have risked everything in order to split the train robbery loot. The fourth and last citizen was a dry goods drummer heading for California. And while he was young and smart enough to have masterminded the train robbery, Longarm could sense that he did not have the courage or imagination to do such a bold and daring crime.

"So it's back to the railroad office," Marshal Packard said as they mushed through the deep snow that lined Cook Street.

"Yeah," Longarm said.

"I'll bet that whoever did it is long gone."

"I disagree."

Marshal Packard's eyebrows lifted in question. "But why?"

"Because," Longarm explained. "The one who masterminded this wouldn't have planned on my shooting his accomplices. That means he'd either have had to risk taking all the cash and going on the run from his accomplices, or he'd still be here waiting to pay them their share."

"I see. If he left, he'd most likely have to double-cross those three and have them on his tail until doomsday."

"Exactly."

"Well," Packard said, as they neared the railroad office, "let's see what we can uncover."

• • •

There were eight train employees to interview and Long-arm did a quick, but thorough job because he was good and well practiced. One after another he eliminated the employees until he came to the conductor who had been nice enough to have given him a first-class coach even though his ticket entitled him only to second-class. Ike Berry was a small, unassuming man with a quick smile and kind blue eyes.

Handing the man his rifle, Longarm said, "Ike, before I begin to ask you a few questions, I want to thank you for the use of your Winchester. I'd have been dead without it."

Ike took the rifle and nodded his head vigorously. "Shoots low just like I told you. Don't it?"

"That's right." Longarm noticed that Ike was sweating profusely. "Have you been working in the back room by a furnace or stove?"

"No sir." Ike wiped his face with his handkerchief. "It just seems kind of warm in this little room. That's all."

It wasn't even close to being warm. In fact, Longarm and Marshal Packard had chosen to wear their coats during the interviews because the heat from the main office just didn't seem to penetrate this smaller one.

Longarm also noticed how Ike's knuckles were white as he gripped the rifle. Maybe he was just naturally nervous, but that hadn't seemed to be the case a few days ago when he'd been so accommodating.

"Ike, how long have you worked as a conductor?"

"About three years."

"That's not very long. I should have thought you'd been employed much longer."

"I used to be a miner," Ike blurted. "I prospected all these mountains but never struck it rich. Then my joints started to give me trouble, so I had to quit and take something that was a bit easier on this old body."

"You're not *that* old."

"I'm fifty-nine, but I've had a rough life."

"Mining is hard and dangerous."

"Yes, sir, it is."

Longarm could almost taste the conductor's fear. Could this small, unassuming man really have been daring and inventive enough to have masterminded the train robbery? It didn't seem possible, but Longarm had learned never to eliminate a man who was acting strange or suspiciously.

"So, Ike, what do you plan to do with your share of the train loot?" Longarm asked nonchalantly.

The conductor blanched and began to stammer. "Marshal, I . . . I didn't steal that money!"

Longarm detected a bald-faced lie. "Sure you did." His voice hardened. "Where *is* the money? If you give it up, it'll go a whole lot easier on you."

"I swear I didn't steal a thing! Marshal Long. Please! I'm too old to go to prison!"

Longarm glanced sideways at Packard. "Do you believe this man?"

"Not anymore."

"Me neither," Longarm said. He reached across the table between himself and Ike Berry and grabbed the conductor by the front of his coat. "You've got only one chance to come clean with me and it's right now. If you continue to hold out and lie . . . I swear that you'll hang for the murder of Jack Slater!"

Ike Berry begin to shake as if he had the ague. His eyes rolled around like marbles in a cup and his face turned the color of a gravestone. "I . . . I wasn't a part of it, Marshal. I swear on the Holy Bible that I didn't have anything to do with that murder."

"Who did?"

"I . . . I just saw her take the gold and cash. That's all. I saw her and she pulled a derringer on me and practically stuck its barrel up my nose. Then she told me that she would either blow out my brains, or give me five hundred dollars of the stolen money if I kept my mouth shut."

"Who are you talking about?"

"Why, that woman you were sleeping with, Marshal Long. Mrs. Irene Hanson!"

Longarm released the man and rocked back in his chair. "*She* was mastermind of the train robbery?"

"I don't know about that, but she was a part of it," Ike answered. "Oh please. I don't want to die. I have a wife in poor health. *I'm* in poor health. Please don't send me to prison or we're both finished."

Then, Ike Berry, the ex-prospector and kindly conductor, broke down and wept like a baby.

"Jesus," Marshal Packard swore softly. "I would never have believed that he was a part of that train holdup."

"He wasn't," Longarm said. "Ike was just a man who happened to see something that almost cost him his life. Then, he was given a choice to either live . . . or die. And he made the only choice a sane man could make. Ike Berry chose to live."

"But he took five hundred dollars!"

"It was payoff money to insure his silence," Longarm patiently explained. "And while he should have handed it over to the authorities at the first possible moment . . ."

"But I did!" Berry cried. "I put it in an envelope with an explanation and mailed it without my name. I couldn't afford to be tied up with a murder."

"If that's true," Longarm said. "Where's the envelope?"

"I don't know. I . . . I sent the five one hundred dollar bills to the railroad headquarters in Denver. Maybe it's there already, but maybe not."

Longarm looked over at Marshal Packard. "Abe, go down to the telegraph office and find out if the money arrived. If it did, I'd recommend we keep this completely to ourselves."

"And not even tell Mr. Olander?"

"If we tell him, then this man will be ruined. He'll lose his job and he'll never be able to hold his head up in this town. Not only will he suffer, but in all likelihood, so will his wife. Do we need for that to happen?" Longarm answered his own question. "I don't think so."

"I agree." Packard came to his feet. "Ike, if you're tellin' us straight, there's no need for you or your wife to suffer. We'll just keep this to ourselves as our little secret."

"Thank you!" the conductor cried.

When Packard left to send the telegram, Longarm fished a bottle of whiskey out of his coat pocket, uncorked and handed it to the conductor. "Take a drink and calm down," he suggested. "If the money arrived in Denver like you said, there is nothing to fear."

"But what if it didn't? What if someone felt the bills and opened the letter and . . ."

Longarm motioned for the rattled man to drink saying, "If that happened, we'll get to the bottom of it. Besides, it's unlikely the money, if properly addressed, failed to reach its destination. So let's just settle down and assume that you are in the clear."

Ike took two long, shuddering gulps of the whiskey and visibly forced himself to relax. "What else can I do to help?" he asked in a raw voice.

"You can tell me exactly what you saw Miss Hanson do."

"I stumbled into the mail room just in time to see the three killers fly out of the car. I saw Mrs. Hanson holding the money and gold in a leather valise. It looked like a doctor's medical kit. Big, black and made of leather."

"I remember that valise," Longarm said. "And I remember that it seemed an odd thing for a woman to carry. I thought it might belong to some man in her life."

"Maybe it did, and maybe it didn't," Ike said. "But anyway, when I stumbled into the coach, the three killers were leaving. If they'd seen me on their way out, do you think they'd have slit my throat like they did poor Jack's?"

"Probably."

The conductor shivered and took another drink of Longarm's whiskey. "I was so shocked and surprised to see the derringer in Mrs. Hanson's fist that I almost died of fright. I had the feeling that she was thinking of killing me and when I looked deep into her eyes, I felt that she was capable of that act. So I just stood in place feeling my bones turn to ice and nearly soiling my pants."

Longarm nodded with understanding. "Go on."

"Like I said, she just looked at me as if I was a rabbit choking in her noose and then she must have decided there was no way that she could fire the derringer without the shot being heard. Either that, or explain my dead body."

"I agree. That's likely what saved your life."

Ike took a deep breath. "Marshal Long. You slept with the woman. Didn't you even once suspect that she . . ."

"No," he said, remembering. "I saved her life in Denver and I thought she was a victim . . . not someone who was planning to rob a train. But I still doubt she intended to have Jack Slater murdered."

"Intended or not," the little conductor said, "she would be an accomplice and be guilty of murder. Wouldn't she?"

"Yes," Longarm grudgingly admitted. "She would."

"What a pity," Ike Berry said. "Earlier on, I even had romantic notions that you and she might fall in love and get married."

"Good thing that didn't happen."

"So what," the conductor asked, "is next?"

"I'll pass along the information, and telegraphs will be sent ahead. With any luck, Mrs. Hanson will be arrested somewhere down the line and sent back here to be tried in Colorado for murder."

Ike Berry nodded. "It must seem . . . especially difficult for you to imagine, Marshal. I mean, given your. . . ."

Longarm cut the man short. "Yes. Now why don't you just go home."

Berry blinked with surprise. "You mean you're trusting me to leave even before Marshal Packard learns if the five hundred dollars arrived in Denver?"

"Sure," Longarm said. "After all, you have a sick wife here and where could you run?"

"No place," Berry flatly stated. "The only way in and out of Raton is on the train."

"That's right, and I'll be on it tomorrow heading for Arizona."

"Is that where Mrs. Hanson said she was going?"

"As a matter of fact, it is." Longarm pried his bottle from Berry's clenched fist and took a drink. "But then, why should I believe anything Irene told me, given what I've just learned?"

"If you catch up with her," Berry warned. "For heaven's sake don't trust her or believe her lies."

"I won't."

The conductor shook his head. "When I looked into her eyes that instant, I swear she was ready to kill me and almost did. Didn't you notice that in her eyes?"

Longarm turned away, not wanting to think about, much less remember his most intimate moments with the beautiful and passionate Irene. Sure he'd looked into her eyes a thousand times in just the short time they'd been traveling together. He'd marveled at their brilliance across the table as they'd dined and sipped wine. And he'd looked down deeply into her eyes at the very moment when she cried out in ecstasy as he filled her with his seed and her body bucked with joyous release.

He hadn't seen a killer any of those times. He'd only seen a very lovely, complicated and passionate young woman.

Chapter 10

Longarm had a six-hour layover in Santa Fe. He departed the train and paid a visit to the telegraph office where he sent a message off to both Billy Vail in Denver as well as Marshal Packard in Raton. His message to Billy was just to inform his boss that he had been detained but was now on his way to Flagstaff to investigate the murder charges against Big Lips.

His telegraph to Marshal Packard was to find out if the five hundred dollars had arrived in Denver as Ike Berry promised. Moments after his message to Packard, a reply came in from Raton assuring him that, indeed, the money from the conductor had arrived. Marshal Packard also said that no one would ever know that Ike Berry had played a reluctant part in the train robbery.

"Good," Longarm said quietly to himself as he tore the message up and threw it in a wastebasket.

"Everything all right with you, Marshal?" the telegraph operator asked.

"It's just fine, but I wonder if you know where I can locate an old lady named Slater. Her son, Jack Slater, was murdered while guarding a mail car on the way over Raton Pass."

"We all heard about that," the man said. "Damned shame. Did they get the killers who killed poor Jack?"

"Yeah," Longarm answered, not bothering to explain that he had been the one to deliver the loggers to their just and final reward.

"That's mighty good news. Did they recover the stolen money and gold from them killers?"

"No. They weren't carrying the stolen cash or gold."

"Any other suspects?"

"Maybe," Longarm said, unwilling to discuss the matter any further. "I'd like to pay Mrs. Slater a visit. Can you tell me where she can be found?"

"She's been moved up to the old folks' home. It's located up on Grant Avenue."

"Just recently?"

"Yes sir. When the telegram arrived telling us that poor Jack was killed guarding the mail car safe, I took the message over to the marshal and he and the Reverend Paulson went straight on over to see Mrs. Slater. She took it real, real hard. Jack was pretty much all she had left in this world and I heard she almost went crazy when she learned her son was murdered."

"Damn," Longarm muttered. "Is she still right in the head?"

"I think so. She's tough. I haven't talked to the marshal here yet but that old lady was real sharp. She was just so weak and upset they didn't trust her to live alone. People here in town are taking up a collection. If you want to contribute, you can do it at the Stockman's Bank or at the Baptist Church on Lincoln Avenue."

"I will," Longarm promised, then asked for directions to the old folks' home.

When he arrived, he discovered that it was a two-story white mansion surrounded by an ornamental fence and a locked iron gate. Longarm rang a little bell and an attractive Mexican woman about fifty years old came out to the gate.

"Can I help you?" she asked.

"I'm Marshal Custis Long and, if she's up to having visitors, I'd like to see Mrs. Slater."

The Mexican woman paused, then asked. "What is the nature of your business?"

"I was on the train when her son was killed. I thought that I might be able to give his mother a few words of comfort."

"Perhaps so. Come on in, Señor."

The gate was unlocked and Longarm was led up a pretty flagstone walk lined by shrubs to the porch of the stately mansion. The Mexican lady turned to him and said, "You must wait here. I will return very soon with Mrs. Slater."

"Señora?"

"Yes?"

"I know that Mrs. Slater has suffered quite a shock. If you think that she might not be up to a visitor or about hearing the name of her son, then . . ."

"She will be glad to hear what you have to say. But no details of the death."

"Of course not." Longarm sure didn't have it in mind to tell Jack's mother that her son had been both shot and had his throat cut from ear to ear.

Longarm found a nice, comfortable chair on the porch and waited about ten minutes. The Mexican woman appeared leading a very old and frail woman with white hair and clear blue eyes. Mrs. Slater used a cane to walk and her skin was as pale as snow. Whatever she had done in her life, Longarm could guess that it had been mostly indoors.

"This is Marshal Long," the Mexican woman said, as she helped the old lady into a seat beside Longarm. "He knew Jack."

Mrs. Slater reached out and placed her thin, blue-veined hand on Longarm's sleeve. "Did you know my son well?"

"I'm afraid not. But I did know him long enough to learn that he was devoted to you, Mrs. Slater. He was on his way down here to be close by your side and he told me that he loved you."

She smiled and her eyes grew moist. "What a wonderful thing for you to tell me."

"Jack was a brave man. I thought you ought to know that he put up a good fight against those robbers."

"Yes, but not quite good enough."

"He was overpowered and taken by surprise."

"Were they apprehended?"

"I tracked them from the train down a mountain and had to shoot them to death."

The old woman's eyes lit up with joy. "Wonderful! That is absolutely the most wonderful thing I've heard in days!"

Her enthusiasm caught Longarm a bit off guard, but he nodded in agreement. "They were three bad characters."

"Only three?"

"Maybe more," Longarm hedged. "In fact, the gold and cash hasn't been recovered and I think there was a woman in cahoots with the three killers."

"A *woman*!"

"Yes, ma'am."

"Then I hope you catch and hang the bloody bitch!"

Longarm blinked with astonishment at the venom he heard in Mrs. Slater's voice. "Yes ma'am." He decided it best to change the subject. "I understand that they're taking up a collection for you here in Santa Fe."

"That's right. Would you be willing to help support a poor old widow whose only family was killed in the line of duty?"

"I sure will."

"How much?" Mrs. Slater demanded, leaning in close.

93

"Ma'am?"

"How *much* money can you afford to give me?"

"Well, I . . ."

Mrs. Slater's lips formed a thin, resolute line and her eyes were penetrating when she announced, "Marshal Long, a hundred dollars would be very much appreciated."

Custis was dumbfounded by her audacity, and it took him a moment to recover enough to stammer, "I'm sorry, but I don't have that much to give. I'm just a federal marshal and we aren't paid that well."

"Better, by far, than Jack was paid as a railroad security guard, I'll bet."

"Well, maybe, but . . ."

The woman's eyes hardened. "What about fifty dollars then? Surely you can give that much to help an old lady whose brave son was just murdered in the flower of his youth."

Longarm wasn't going to argue or dicker. Jack Slater had been far removed from "the flower of his youth" but Longarm thought it unwise to mention that salient fact. And since the old lady was sticking out her bony little fingers curled and grasping for cash, he gave her fifty dollars, which she deftly folded and slipped up into her lacy sleeve.

"Thank you, Marshal Long," she said sweetly. "Are you staying in Santa Fe?"

"No ma'am," Longarm replied, realizing that now he'd have to wire Billy Vail for more travel money. "I'm headed for Arizona."

"Are you going after that horrible woman who plotted to rob and murder my son?"

"Yes, ma'am."

"Good! When you catch her I hope she swings!"

"She might."

"Prison is too good for one like that," Mrs. Salter declared, fists clenched in anger. "Catch her, Marshal Long. Catch and hang her and then cut off a nice, thick lock of her hair and send it straight to me at this address."

Longarm didn't understand. "What . . ."

Mrs. Slater's face twisted with hatred and fury. "Because I'll sprinkle that bitch's hair in my chamber pot and then I'll *piss* on it!"

Longarm decided it was time to go. He excused himself and didn't look back but he could hear the old woman cackling. Maybe, he decided, her mind had cracked after all.

Three days and one bad New Mexico snowstorm later, Longarm arrived in Flagstaff, Arizona. The temperature was just a shade above freezing, but there wasn't any snow on the ground. As was his custom, he immediately went to see the local marshal to inform the man of his presence and intention to investigate the murders surrounding Big Lips Lilly Cameron.

Marshal Pete Pitman was a slow-moving and slow-talking man in his early fifties, who looked as if he hadn't bathed or shaved in a week. He stood about six feet tall and probably weighed nearly three hundred pounds, most of it fat. His appearance was sloppy and unkempt and his office was littered with newspapers, dirty dishes, unwashed coffee cups and other articles of discarded trash. Longarm formed an immediate dislike and distrust of the man and wondered how he'd ever gotten elected to office.

"I don't much appreciate the federal government pokin' its nose into local business."

"A federal judge was murdered," Longarm reminded the law officer. "That gives us the right to conduct a full investigation."

"Waste of government money," Pitman declared, jabbing his finger in Longarm's direction so often that he wanted to reach out an break it. "Federal government sure likes to waste the taxpayers' money. How much they pay you a month?"

Pitman chuckled so that his multiple chins wiggled. "You're a tall, testy one, ain't ya? Well, it don't matter to me what you do or say. Big Lips is gonna hang in about ten days and that's the end of *that* story. Be a big time in town when she does swing. Lots of boys gonna watch her pretty legs kickin' at the sky and wish they was wrapped around their necks. Big Lips is a looker, in case you haven't heard."

"I heard. And I'd like to see her immediately."

"Ain't possible."

"Why not?"

The marshal stabbed a fat finger in Longarm's direction. "Big Lips is being held to await a public hanging in Williams."

"Why?"

Pitman slapped his fat knee and chortled. "Them boys over there nailed planks across the sliding door of a box car and made it into a *jail*."

"She's being held in a box car in this freezing mountain weather?"

"Big Lips is tough. And do you know what else?"

"No."

"My guess is that she'll probably swing sooner than expected."

Longarm fought down the impulse to grab the man and shake him like a water gourd. Instead, he asked, "Why do you say that?"

"Because they have some boys over in Williams that like to take matters into their own hands. Impatient boys that know how to toss a rope over a telegraph pole or pine tree and then what to do with that rope, if you catch my meaning."

"I do," Longarm said, knowing he'd heard just about

as much from this fat lout as he could stand. "Tell me one more thing?"

"Sure, Marshal."

"Is your counterpart in Williams as pathetic as you are?"

Pitman's eyes narrowed and his lips curled down at the corners. "You federal people are all alike. You think you know better than anyone else what needs to be done. But you don't. My advice to you is to get back on the train and return to Denver."

"Your advice is worth what I paid for it," Longarm said, heading for the door. "It's worth nothing."

Pitman shouted something uncomplimentary at Longarm as the door was closing, but it wasn't worth the effort to go back and teach the fat man a lesson in civility, so Longarm kept walking.

He needed to get to Williams and speak to Big Lips who was locked like an animal in some freezing railroad boxcar. And, judging from what he'd just been told about the vigilantes in that town, he needed to get there quick.

Chapter 11

Longarm was feeling miffed when he plowed out of the Flagstaff marshal's office. He was certain that the fat, slothful lawman wouldn't have a clue as to the disappearance of Miss Irene Hanson. But perhaps the local newspaper office knew of the infamous woman and her late husband . . . if that part of the story all hadn't been a lie.

When he stepped into the newspaper office, Longarm saw a man about his own age wearing a green eyeshade bent over a copy of his newly printed edition.

"Excuse me," Longarm said, interrupting the man's concentration. "Could I have a minute of your time?"

"Sure," the editor replied, removing his eyeshade and giving Longarm a tired smile. "Especially if you're interested in paying for some advertising."

"I'm afraid not."

"Oh well. How about purchasing a copy of the latest edition? It only costs ten cents and it's worth every penny."

"I'd like that," Longarm replied, reaching into his pocket and dredging up a dime. "But what I'm really in-

98

terested in is if you know anything about a woman named Irene Hanson."

"Nope. Does she live here?"

"I'm not sure where she lives. Maybe down in Prescott."

"Well, I can't help you on that one." The editor collected the dime, dropped it in a tin cup on his desk and started to go back to work. "Enjoy your copy."

"I'm a federal marshal sent here from Denver to investigate the murder trial of Miss Lilly Cameron. I'd appreciate it if you could you give me a little information?"

"Sure, Marshal. But it'll cost you."

"How much?"

"Not money. I run a good newspaper here and the people are very interested in Big Lips Lilly. To some she's a saint, to others a harlot and a murderer. Whatever I write about the woman sells copies and selling print is what keeps me in business. So I'd like your promise that you keep me abreast of whatever it is that you came to find out."

"I can't promise you anything," Longarm said. "I'm here to do an investigation into Miss Cameron's guilt . . . or innocence."

"Haven't you heard that she's already been tried and found guilty by old Judge Taylor?"

"I didn't know the judge's name but I knew she was found guilty of murdering former Governor Lance Wilder. And I'd heard that they were married secretly before he took office."

"That's right. It turns out that Governor Wilder had a lot of skeletons in his closet . . . though I'd never call Big Lips a skeleton. But it was brought out in court that they had married and Judge Taylor ruled that she had killed the governor by hiring an assassin."

This was news to Longarm. "What was this assassin's name?"

"No one knows and he was never identified or found."

Longarm scowled. "Then how could Taylor sentence Big Lips to the gallows?"

"A letter turned up in now Governor Stanton Pennington's office. In the letter, the assassin confessed to killing Wilder. The assassin's letter contained a second letter that he said was sent to him along with blood money from Big Lips."

"He said that she was the one who paid him to kill then Governor Lance Wilder?"

"That's right."

"Was the letter in her handwriting?" Longarm asked, thinking it odd that anyone would be foolish enough to send a letter that could be used against them in a court of law.

"The letter was indeed written in Big Lips Lilly's own handwriting. And, Marshal, it was as cold-blooded an order as you could imagine. Big Lips wrote that she'd been jilted by Wilder and she wanted to get even and teach him a lesson. She said right in the letter that she included one hundred dollars in earnest money and would add an additional one hundred dollars when the assassin's work was done."

"I see. But this assassin never showed his face and was never seen or identified in any way?"

"No sir. But the letter was written in Big Lips's hand."

"There are plenty of criminals skilled at forgery."

"And with her stationery?"

"It could have been stolen," Longarm argued.

"Yes, the letter could have been a fraud and someone could have gotten their hands on Big Lips's stationery. But the fact of the matter is that the woman was heard to have threatened Governor Wilder's life on many occasions. Big Lips hated him and made her feelings very public."

Longarm shrugged. "Why would someone who had

100

publicly threatened her ex-husband with murder actually commit the murder unless they were an idiot?"

"Not ex-husband," the newspaper editor corrected. "They were still married when Wilder was gunned down. *And*," he said, emphasizing the point, "they had a will and it stated that, if either died, all their assets were to go to the other."

"And I suppose that Governor Wilder had considerable assets."

"You bet he did! Not that Big Lips was exactly destitute. She had a hefty bank account, but it didn't equal that of the Governor."

"All right," Longarm conceded. "Lilly Cameron had motive and there's this matter of her letter sent to the assassin. But it still seems to me pretty circumstantial."

"It didn't to Judge Taylor. And don't forget that a federal judge was found murdered and the evidence again pointed to Big Lips Lilly Cameron."

"Evidence enough to convict her of that murder?"

"Listen," the newspaper man said. "It is a known fact that Big Lips killed two men in Williams. There were witnesses that saw her shoot one and stab the other."

"I heard about that and it seems to me that the woman was defending her life. Wasn't she badly beaten?"

"Yes."

"Since when is self-defense considered murder?"

"Look," the editor said, offering Longarm a tolerant smile. "I know what you are thinking."

"No you don't."

"Yes I do," the man countered. "Everyone who hears the saga of Big Lips Lilly Cameron quickly jumps on one side of the band wagon or the other—she's either a saint or a sinner. Innocent or guilty."

"She spent two years in the Yuma Prison for the murders of those men who were beating her. That sounds to me like heavy-handed justice for fighting for her life."

"She wasn't exactly fighting for her life when she killed those men," the newspaper man said. "In fact, one of them was trying to escape when she shot him in the back of the head. Unfortunately, the one that she stabbed was the son of a prominent Williams businessman. The young man had a wife and family."

"But he liked to frequent brothels and beat up women," Longarm snapped.

"Well," the newspaper man said, "I have to agree that neither man was a model of propriety. In fact, they'd both been in a lot of trouble with the law—mostly for drunk and disorderly conduct but also for assault and battery."

"There you have it," Longarm said. "So Judge Taylor sentenced Big Lips to two years in that hellish Yuma prison. And I suppose she came out pretty hard and bitter."

"That's what I've heard. Marshal, Big Lips has always been an outspoken rebel. Like I said, you either love her or hate her, but nothing in between. Well, this time, the evidence seemed enough to Judge Taylor that she should receive the death penalty. And that's exactly what she was given."

"I'm going to visit her and Judge Taylor," Longarm said, preparing to leave. "A letter sent by an anonymous assassin doesn't seem to be substantial enough evidence to warrant the death penalty."

"It did to Judge Taylor." The newspaper owner sighed. "But in fairness to Big Lips, I'll tell you what I think."

"And that is?"

"I think the woman got a raw deal. I think because she operated brothels in Northern Arizona and became wealthy, a lot of so-called upstanding citizens were outraged. Furthermore, they were still mad about being deceived by Governor Wilder, who swore that he was a bachelor when he was elected to office but was in fact secretly married to Big Lips Lilly. People everywhere take it very personal when they've been lied to."

"Sure they do," Longarm said. "But that isn't reason enough to pervert the law and hang an innocent person."

"Maybe not, but that's the way it is going to happen."

"Don't be too sure of that," Longarm said. "And thanks for all the inside information."

"I don't want your thanks, Marshal. I want the story if it turns out that the death sentence was in error. Or, even better, if you uncover evidence that proves that Big Lips is innocent not only of murdering Governor Wilder, but also the federal judge."

Longarm picked up his newspaper. "I'll give you first crack at it if I find out anything interesting."

"If you're in Williams or Prescott, just wire me and I'll pay the charges."

"I'll keep that in mind," Longarm told the man as he was going out the door.

On his way out, Longarm bumped into none other than Marshal Pitman. Since he neither liked nor respected the local law officer, Longarm said nothing in greeting but started to step around the big man. Pitman, however, blocked his path on the boardwalk.

"Marshal," Longarm said, "it's going to be pretty embarrassing if I have to pitch your fat ass out into the street."

"You could try," Pitman said. "But you might be the one that ends up lying out there among the horse turds. I see that you were visiting Mr. Tiller."

"If that's the name of your editor, then you're correct."

"And I suppose that he gave you his opinion on Big Lips?"

"What we talked about is none of your business."

"I'm making it my business. What did he say? That Big Lips is innocent?"

"I'll tell you one more time, Pitman. What we talked about is none of your business."

103

"It is my business and by gawd I'm going to go in there and have a word or two with Mr. Tiller. I'm sick and tired of his editorials and the way he's always insulting me and the other elected town officials!"

Longarm grabbed the marshal's arm. "If I hear that you have given Mr. Tiller any grief, I'm going to come back here and make you eat his newspaper."

Pitman spat into the street. "I don't like you and I'm warning you to get on the train and get out of my town."

"It isn't *your* town, Pitman. It belongs to the people, although I can't, for for the life of me imagine how they could have elected you to the office of town marshal."

"Get out of Flagstaff before I throw you in my jail!"

Longarm had taken just about enough from this huge tub of lard. "Step aside or I'll take you apart right in front of the people you are supposed to protect."

"You touch me and I'll see that you go first to my jail and then to prison," Pitman hissed. "You're just a federal marshal. Arizona is a territory and we know to how to handle our own problems without you feds stickin' your noses in our business."

Longarm could have drawn his gun and cracked Pitman across the head and then kicked him into the street to lie in the mud, but instead he slammed the heel of his boot down hard on the town marshal's toe. Pitman wasn't expecting that; he cried out in pain, lifting one foot. That's when Longarm gave the fat man a tremendous shove that sent him flying off the boardwalk to land on his back in the mud.

Pitman was pathetic. He wasn't even wearing a gun and his pitiful tirade brought smiles from everyone who saw the sad spectacle of the marshal clumsily trying to regain his feet.

Longarm walked on down to the railroad depot. He hoped that he would never have to see such a sorry excuse for a lawman again. With luck, Pitman's counterpart in both Williams and Prescott would be far more professional.

At the train depot, Longarm asked what appeared to be a local businessman, "How did you ever wind up with such a bad town marshal?"

The man's jaw muscles tightened. "We didn't vote him in, that's for sure."

"Well then what. . . ."

"Marshal Pitman had just been hired by the former marshal when the man was gunned down. We had another deputy, but he was so scared he ran away and that left Pitman. We'll run him out of office before long."

"The sooner, the better," Longarm told the man. "By the way, I'm a federal marshal. My name is Custis Long."

The man was wearing a nice suit, tie and gold watch with chain. "My name is Raymond Craft. I am a banker and investor. What are you doing in our town?"

"I came to investigate the murder charges against Lilly Cameron."

"Ah yes, Big Lips. Well, Marshal Long, she is guilty as sin and twice as tempting."

"Is that right?"

"It is," Craft said with authority. "The woman is a cold-blooded killer without conscience."

"I've heard others judge her differently."

"She has her fans."

Longarm nodded. "And obviously, you're not one of them."

"Hardly."

"Were you ever one of her customers?"

The banker blanched. "Why . . . why of course not!"

"Oh?"

"Marshal, I resent . . ."

"All aboard!" shouted the conductor. "Next stop is Williams, Arizona. Time of arrival is one hour and ten minutes. All aboard!"

Longarm climbed back onto the train and took a seat by the window knowing full well that the banker had been a customer at one of Big Lips's brothels. What else would explain his over-reaction and offended outrage? Maybe personal guilt was one of the primary reasons that people wanted to hang the former madam.

He could look up Flagstaff's main street all the way through the town. And up at the other end, he saw that there was quite a commotion taking place.

"Probably Pitman still trying to get his fat fanny out of the mud," Longarm muttered as the train whistle blasted and the train jolted forward headed for Williams and his long anticipated meeting with Big Lips Lilly.

Chapter 12

Williams, Arizona, was named after the famous mountain man Bill Williams and it was a railroad, timber and ranching area. Smaller than either Flagstaff or Prescott, the community nevertheless had a prosperous and independent attitude, which was apparent the moment Longarm stepped off the train.

"Marshal, you might just want to be careful what you do and say here," the conductor warned. "This is a town that pretty much takes the law into its own hands."

"Doesn't it have a marshal?"

"Not really," the conductor replied. "They do have a mayor who doubles as a constable. And, of course, there is the all-powerful city council, composed mostly of businessmen. Pretty much what the mayor and town council say is law here and I never got the feeling that they wanted to give up any of their authority."

Longarm collected his luggage. "I've been through here before on my way west but I've never stopped for more than an hour. This always seemed like a peaceful town."

"Oh it is," the conductor said, "except on Saturday nights or when some fool comes in here looking for trouble. But lately, Williams is all astir over Big Lips's upcoming hanging. That's pretty much all you'll hear talked about in the saloons and on the streets."

"Where is her boxcar serving as a jail?"

The conductor pointed to a rail siding and a large boxcar where three or four well-bundled-up ladies were gathered at the opening. "That's it, Marshal."

Longarm took a deep breath of the thin, cold mountain air. "I don't think it's right that a prisoner should be confined where anyone can come and stare at them like they were caged animals."

"Aw," the man said, "don't fret too much about that. I went over to take a peek at Big Lips myself during our last stop. She doesn't seem to mind all the attention."

"Is that a fact?"

"It is," the conductor assured him. "Part of the boxcar is walled off inside so she has some privacy and the bleeding hearts insisted that she have a potbellied stove, so they cut a hole in the back side of the car and put a stove pipe through the opening. I dunno. When you visit Big Lips, you won't hear her complain."

Longarm headed up the railroad siding noticing how the supporters of Big Lips had built stairs leading up to a large wooden platform. The platform was positioned in front of the boxcar's large open door, which was now laced with timbers across the front so closely spaced that only a child could have squeezed through and escaped.

"What a side show," he muttered.

When Longarm arrived at the boxcar, he said loud enough to be heard by everyone on the platform, "My name is Marshal Custis Long and I've been sent from Denver to investigate the murder charges against this woman. I'm going to need to speak to her in private, so you ladies need to say goodbye and clear out."

The women's glares were cold and suspicious. One said, "We've lost faith in the law and I doubt you've come here to restore that faith. Marshal Long, why don't you just go off somewhere and . . . and play with your gun!"

Her remark caused the others to titter. Longarm flushed with anger and embarrassment. He showed them his badge and said, "Git, while I speak with Miss Cameron."

The woman threw up her nose and turned to the boxcar. "Lilly, do you want to speak to this lawman or should we make a big fuss?"

"I think I'll speak to him just in case he means well," came the voice. "But stay close in case he really intends to poke his gun through these boards and murder me."

Longarm overheard those words and had a few of his own. "I'm sworn to uphold the law and I sure don't intend to murder anyone."

"Humph!" the leader snorted. "We've seen what the so-called law does and we don't have any faith left in justice."

"Move," Longarm growled, his patience at an end.

The women marched down the stairs and then off about fifty yards where they folded their arms in their shawls and watched Longarm's every move as he climbed the stairs to visit the infamous former madam, now accused and convicted of murdering not one, but four different men.

The interior of the boxcar was well illuminated because Lilly had a pair of lanterns hanging on the walls. Longarm was also surprised to see rugs on the rough wooden floor planks. There were even a few articles of nice furniture in addition to a bed that was covered with a thick bearskin rug.

"Well," he said, "it's almost like traveling in first-class coach."

"Yes," Lilly agreed, coming up to study his face, "but the bad part is that the destination is that gallows."

She stuck her hand through the planks and pointed to a gallows which Longarm hadn't noticed because his attention had been so focused on this boxcar. It was a gallows all right, and someone had even supplied it with a hangman's noose that now dangled and swayed in the breeze.

"It sort of takes the fun out of life," Lilly told him. "Marshal, have you hanged a lot of men?"

"Nary a one."

"Oh really?"

"But I have seen a good many swing."

"Do they suffer horribly?" Big Lips asked, unable to hide the tremor in her voice.

"If the hangman does his work properly, when they hit the end of the rope their necks are broken and I doubt they suffer at all."

"But what if the hangman botches the job?"

"Listen," Longarm said, not wanting to carry this line of conversation any further, "why . . ."

"Answer my question!" Big Lips said sharply. "What happens if the hangman botches the job?"

"I'm afraid that the condemned person chokes to death," Longarm answered.

"That would be pretty awful, wouldn't it?"

"Yes. It's not a sight that any decent person ought to witness and it's one that will stay with you forever."

"Marshal," she said, her voice subdued, "thank you for being honest. It means I might even be able to trust you."

Big Lips must have been crouching slightly because now she stood to her full height so that her face was clearly visible between the cross planks. Longarm had expected her to be pretty, but hard as a result of her two year stay in the Yuma Prison. But he was wrong. Big Lips's face was pale but unlined, mature but still youthful. Her lips were full but they weren't excessively large. Her hair was golden and her eyes were as clear as the overhead mountain sky. She wore a black velvet dress, gold earrings and bracelets on both wrists.

"Marshal," she said, coming close enough that he could

110

smell her heady French perfume, "you can tell me what you really came here for when you're done gawkin' and you're ready to do some talkin'."

Longarm wasn't in the habit of staring at women, but Big Lips was worth the effort. "Excuse me. I'd heard you were pretty, but that word does you a great injustice."

"You're not so bad yourself," she said with a wide smile. "Say, Marshal, how come a big, handsome man like you hasn't done better for himself than to become a lawman?"

"I like what I do."

"You like tracking down outlaws and sending people to the gallows?"

Longarm shrugged.

Big Lips shook her head and started to turn away. "Then I don't think we have a thing to talk about. Call back my friends."

"Wait a minute," he protested. "I came all the way from Denver to see if you might be innocent."

"Sure you did," Big Lips said, not bothering to hide her sarcasm. "What I suspect you came for was to see what all the other men who are so eager to watch me swing hope to see."

"And that would be?"

"A free peek at what only the best and most fortunate of men were allowed to pay for."

"Hangings aren't my favorite pastimes," he told her. "I'd rather see justice done."

"Sure you would."

"I'm serious, and so are the people who sent me all the way out here to Arizona. We want to know if you really killed Governor Wilder and that federal judge."

"The judge's name was Otto. Maxwell Otto and he was a swine. He paid well though, so I put up with him for a while. When he got to be intolerable, I gave him to one of my better girls. Maxwell was offended. He became more than intolerable. He became dangerous and insanely jealous."

"So one of your girls killed him?"

"He was beating her and she stabbed him to death in self-defense. But that's always a hanging offense for women in this part of the country, so I sent the girl away in order to save her life."

"And you took the blame?"

"No one had any proof, but they pinned the murder on me anyway. It happened in my brothel, so I was held responsible and that's why I've been sentenced to hang."

"You could save yourself by telling me the name of the girl. If she testified that she stabbed Judge Otto in self-defense, the jury would not only set her free, but you as well."

"You're wrong. I know the people of this town far better than you do, Marshal. Mostly likely, we'd both hang. So it's better that I just keep my mouth shut and go it alone."

"Could you at least tell a judge or jury the real circumstances?"

Big Lips shook her head. "Everyone would just accuse me of trying to save my own life by putting the blame on someone else. What I did say in court was that Judge Otto was corrupt and a pig. He had some good men hanged simply because they wouldn't pay him under the table."

"Serious charges."

"I know. And I can't prove it to you any more than I could prove it to a judge. But it's the truth."

"Look," Longarm persisted, "if you told me in private the name of your girl who stabbed the judge, I could at least find her and try to . . ."

"Give it up, Marshal. She is a good friend and she'd go to prison or hang. So let's not talk about that anymore because it will get me mad and you nowhere. Agreed?"

Longarm wasn't accustomed to being talked to like this,

especially by a person he was trying to save from the gallows. "All right. Will you tell me about Governor Wilder?"

"He was a pig of a different color."

"That's not what I've heard."

"Sure. You heard he was handsome, eloquent and intelligent. That he was what the politicians call a 'comer,' which has an entirely different connotation in my former business."

"And he wasn't?"

Big Lips scoffed. "He was all those things, but he was rotten to the core. Did you know that he was a professional gambler most of his life before he stepped into politics?"

"Yes. And I also know that you were married."

"Well, big deal! Everyone knows that and it created the biggest scandal seen in Arizona in many a year. What they *didn't* know was that Lance was terribly addicted to opium."

"Is that right?"

"Sure is. Opium was what he craved and he'd go to the Chinese opium dens and lose himself. They'd keep him under wraps for days while he drifted in a cloudy haze. However, if opium wasn't available, whiskey and sex would carry him until he got to the Chinese dens. He was a flawed man, Marshal Long. But then, I've come to understand that we're all flawed . . . but men usually far more than women."

Longarm said nothing because he realized why the condemned woman held such a jaundiced point of view.

Big Lips leaned forward until her head was resting on the timbers that served as bars to her makeshift jail. "So what are *your* flaws?"

Longarm smiled. "I have many, but I damn sure didn't come all the way from Denver through a blizzard and a murder to make a confession about myself."

"A blizzard and a murder? Whose ticket got punched?"

"A railroad security guard. His neck was slashed on Raton Pass. He left a mother in Santa Fe who, it turns out, was probably sharper and tougher than he was."

"Well, I'm glad to hear that. Sometimes I think that there are already way too many men running around the West." She chuckled at her own observation. "I'm sure you don't agree, but I'll bet the Indians share my opinion."

"Probably so."

"I know so," Big Lips assured him. "I have a lot of Indian friends. Haulapai. Havasupai. Navajo. Hopi. They're all very spiritual people. Are you spiritual, Marshal Long?"

"I don't know. Depends on your definition."

She laughed. "When I drop through the gallows door and my neck snaps, I'll find spirituality and you can bet your badge that it'll be a whole lot finer than what I've seen on this earthly plane."

"You sound like someone who has experienced the worst of life. However, you're wearing expensive gold jewelry and I understand you're a wealthy woman. So why are you so cynical and embittered?"

"Wouldn't you be if you were wrongly sentenced to die?"

"Of course." Longarm reached into his pocket and withdrew a cigar. Lighting it, he said, "Tell me your version and how you were framed by a forged letter?"

"Who filled you in about the letter?"

"A Mr. Tiller who is the newspaper editor over in Flagstaff."

"Aw, yes, poor, sweet Arnie Tiller. The man who wanted to be the next Mark Twain or at least Dan De Quille but never quite cut the literary mustard."

"What about the incriminating letters?" Longarm asked.

"One was from the assassin and the other was from you

to that same assassin. It was written in your hand and on your stationery, and it stated the terms of payment for the murder of Wilder."

Big Lips shook her head. "The letters were bogus. The one from the so-called 'assassin' was probably written by Stanton Pennington."

"And the one on your stationery, written in your hand?"

"Stanton spent many nights with me in my room. He could easily have stolen a few sheets of my stationery and samples of my handwriting. I have always been a letter writer and sometimes I start a letter, don't like the way it's going and toss it in the wastebasket. I'm sure that he took some samples of my handwriting and my stationery and used it to send me to the gallows."

"But you have no way of proving that?"

"No. Marshal Long, what happened in court was exactly what Stanton expected . . . it would be his word against mine. Who is going to believe a madam over their territorial governor?"

Longarm scowled. "So what can I do to try and bring truth to this mess and save your lovely neck?"

Big Lips laughed, but it was not a happy laugh. "Do you really think it is a lovely neck?"

"Of course, and I'd like to see it stay that way."

Tears filled the woman's eyes. "Marshal, I'm starting to believe that you really *are* a good lawman. But the truth is that you can't do a bloomin' thing to save my life. I've had a lot of time in here to mull over every possible way I could keep from marching up the gallows steps and there isn't any way."

"There is, if you tell me who *really* stabbed Judge Max Otto."

"I told you I won't do that because then we might both hang."

"It's your only hope. And . . ."

"Drop it!"

Longarm could see that further argument was useless. Big Lips was bound to protect her friend even if it meant putting her head in the hangman's noose.

"I'll be back later," he said, deciding it was time to leave.

"Can't we talk about something pleasant?"

"No," he told her. "There's nothing pleasant to discuss between us. I came a long way hoping you might be saved and you're unwilling to give me any help. So I guess I'll just have to dig up what I can on my own."

"Forget what I said about one of my girls stabbing Judge Otto to death. It was a lie. I stabbed him to death with my own knife."

"No, you didn't," Longarm said. "And I'm going to find out that girl's name."

"Please just leave it be."

"I can't," Longarm said, preparing to leave. "I'm a lawman sworn to protect the innocent and see that the guilty are punished. I'm convinced that you're innocent of the crime for which you've been sentenced to hang. That means I have no choice but to try to save your life . . . even against your own wishes."

"You'll never find her."

"I can try."

"Starting where?"

Longarm was caught off guard by the question. The truth was he hadn't put much thought to it yet. He'd assumed that Big Lips Lilly Cameron would be desperate to save her own life and willing to do or say just about anything. Now, he momentarily found himself at a loss for words.

"Would you like a hint?" she asked.

"About where to start trying to find that girl? The one that really stabbed Judge Otto to death?"

"No. About how to get to the bottom of this mess. To find out the truth?"

"Of course."

"Stanton Pennington is the Territorial Governor. He lives in a mansion down in Prescott. He keeps himself surrounded by toughs and lackeys and you won't find it easy to get to him, but he holds the key. He's the one that set me up, had that letter forged or forged it himself. He's the man who really ought to be locked in this boxcar."

"Is he married?"

"Yes. But that didn't stop him from coming to visit me whenever he had the chance." Big Lips shook her head. "Stanton likes the ladies. He always wanted the best and the most. That's why he wanted me. If you can get someone on the inside to talk about Stanton, then you might work a crack in the man's armor. But I'm warning you, the man is ruthless. More ruthless than I am, and that's saying something."

"You're not that ruthless," Longarm argued. "If you were, then you'd sell your friend down the river and she'd be fixin' to hang instead of you. And I'll tell you something else. I admire loyalty . . . but yours is blind."

"The girl is blood!" Big Lips cried.

Longarm frowned and gripped the timbers that stood between them. "What does that mean?"

"Never mind," Big Lips told him, moving deeper into the box car and then sitting down in an upholstered chair.

Longarm knew he wasn't going to get any more out of the ex-madam. He was angry, frustrated and just plain puzzled. But he had a week until Big Lips was supposed to hang and he meant to make the very most of it, starting with Stanton Pennington.

Chapter 13

Opening the office door, Longarm stepped inside and said to the man at the desk, "I'd like to see the Mayor of Williams."

The man had been working on some papers. He was in his thirties, short but with a thick neck, arms and bull shoulders. Like Longarm, he wore a handlebar mustache, but also a curly goatee. His brown hair was long on the sides but already thinning on top.

"And what is your business?" he asked, looking up from his papers and carefully laying down his ink pen.

"It's confidential," Longarm answered. "He glanced over the man's head at an office with a metal plaque on the door that read, JOHN R. MILBURN, MAYOR AND CONSTABLE.

"In that case, sit down and tell me what's on your mind."

"Then you're John Milburn?"

"That's right. And you are?"

Longarm introduced himself and when Milburn asked to see his badge, he dragged that out of his pocket. The mayor studied it for a moment then said, "Why aren't you wearing it?"

"Because it's not my style."

"What is your style, Marshal Long?"

"Mind if I have a seat?"

"Help yourself," Milburn said. "But I'm afraid I don't have much time. I have to get these papers on the train so they'll reach Prescott by this evening."

"I'm going to catch the train to Prescott," Longarm said. "And I'll be happy to deliver them."

"No offense, but no thanks."

Longarm had the distinct impression that Milburn either didn't trust him because he was a federal marshal or he didn't like him for the same reason. Either way, it wasn't going to make talking to the man any easier.

"What can I do for you, Marshal?"

"I want to know why Miss Cameron is being locked up in a boxcar like a steer ready for the slaughterhouse."

"Interesting comparison."

"I don't find it as interesting as I do troubling," Longarm said. "It's not acceptable; and putting the boxcar just across from the gallows is more than backward and cruel—it's sadistic."

Milburn's cheeks reddened with anger. "Mister," he said, pointing a finger across his desk, "we don't appreciate strangers coming into Williams telling us we're sadistic or backward."

"You forgot cruel and I don't give a damn what you do or do not appreciate. Furthermore, I have the authority to remove the condemned woman from that boxcar and, if necessary, relocate her, even if that means taking her down to Prescott under my protection."

Milburn came right out of his office chair and his voice shook with fury. "You try that and you won't get the first board pulled off that boxcar before someone puts a bullet in your back."

"Are you threatening me?" Longarm's own temper was on the rise. And even though he knew that he needed this man's cooperation, he was prepared to act with necessary force.

"I'm warning you, Marshal Long. We will not tolerate federal interference. And I don't for one moment believe you have any jurisdiction over our affairs in the matter of Big Lips Cameron."

"We can go to the telegraph office right now and send off a message to Denver or even Washington D.C., and I'll have proof of my authority. How about it, Mayor? Are we going to work with or against each other?"

Their eyes locked in a steely gaze and it was Milburn who finally looked away. Taking a deep breath, he said, "Miss Cameron has a lot of friends here and she asked the town to keep her in that boxcar. Did you visit her yet?"

"I did."

"And were there a good many women vistors?"

"Yes."

"They are her friends. Some of them were her employees in the brothels Lilly operated. She doesn't want to be relocated to Prescott because she fears she will be assassinated even before her hanging date."

"Who would do such a thing?"

"Figure it out, Marshal."

"Stanton Pennington?"

Milburn picked up his ink pen. "I didn't say that name . . . you did. Now, why are you meddling in our affairs?"

"Because I think there is a good chance she is innocent."

"Big Lips is a confirmed killer. She went to the Yuma Prison for . . ."

Longarm cut the man off. "I know about that and I was told she killed in self-defense."

"That's not what the judge and jury decided."

"Let's stop sparring," Longarm said. "Are you intent on seeing the woman hang?"

"I am, because that is the sentence that was given and I feel bound to carry it out. I also feel bound to see that she is well fed and protected until the date of her hanging. Take her down to Prescott and I guarantee you that Big Lips wouldn't last two days before you'd find her either shot, stabbed, throttled or poisoned."

Longarm got up and paced back and forth for a moment. "All right," he said. "I'll go down to Prescott and see if I can dig up some evidence that proves Big Lips didn't kill the federal judge or Governor Wilder."

"Good luck."

Longarm turned to leave and then stopped and said, "By the way, do you know a woman named Mrs. Irene Hanson? Her husband's name was Charlie. Charlie Hanson?"

"Any reason I should know him?"

"Not really. I met his wife, who told me they lived in Prescott and operated a successful freighting business."

"Never heard of it or him."

"Figures," Longarm said, unable to hide his bitterness.

"Something you should tell me, Marshal?"

"No. I don't trust you yet."

"The feeling is mutual." Milburn stood up. He was taller than Longarm had judged and stood almost six feet. The mayor had the look of someone who had been pushing around something a lot heavier than pencils, pens and papers most of his life. "Marshal Long, are you going to try to pin the murders on the Governor?"

"No. But I am going to try and see if he knows more than he's telling."

"You won't get anywhere in Prescott. Our governor is surrounded by protectors and they'll shield you away from him."

"Wrong. I'll speak to the man and, when I do, I'll know if he's telling me the truth."

"How?"

Longarm thought about it a moment. "If you were a *real* lawman and had been at the game as long as I have, you'd know the answer to your own question."

"Is that a fact?"

"It is," Longarm said, getting out of his chair.

"I assume you talked to Big Lips?"

"That's right."

Milburn nodded. "And, of course, she told you she was innocent and that the real killer was the Governor who either forged that letter written on her stationery, or else had someone else forge it."

"Yes."

"Marshal, Big Lips Lilly is the smoothest liar and con artist in Arizona. If it were freezing outside she could convince you it was hot. If it was blistering hot she'd talk you into putting on your overcoat. So don't be suckered into her story and fall for her line. If you do, you'll just be one of many."

"Including yourself?"

Mayor Milburn blushed and Longarm knew he'd struck a tender nerve. No doubt John Milburn had also fallen for Big Lips at some time in the past and now hated her for the damage that relationship had done to either his conscience or his reputation. Once more, Longarm felt he was seeing one of the condemned madam's former lovers out to rid himself of the source of his guilt.

"Hold on," Milburn said, as Longarm moved toward the door. "I'm finishing this letter and I've got to go over to the train depot and see that it's sent. We might as well walk along together."

"Why? Haven't we finished our conversation?"

"Perhaps not."

Longarm didn't know what that was supposed to mean, but it didn't matter to him if the Mayor of Williams walked him to the train depot.

• • •

"We're prospering here," Milburn said as they walked up Fourth Street heading north to the train depot. "When I came here five years ago, the town was in a real slump. Most of the businesses were boarded up and those that weren't looked mighty poor."

"So what changed everything?"

"I did. I went to the Santa Fe and offered them some free land to build a roundhouse. When they balked at that, and said they did all their repair work either in Flagstaff or Ash Fork, I told them that we'd not only give them free land, but we'd build them a new depot and offices. They must have thought I was crazy. I know the townfolks did when I told them of my offer. Hell, I hadn't even asked the city council, because I knew they'd poormouth the deal."

"So how'd you get them to change their minds?"

"I called in then Governor Lance Wilder. He arrived on the train, took one look at the sad situation here and called not only the city council but also the whole damn town to a meeting. And then he laid it on the line and told them that this town was going to dry up and blow away if we didn't do what I'd offered for the Santa Fe. He convinced everyone that we had no choice but to donate the land, build a depot and offices. And by gawd, that's exactly what we did do."

"And Williams was saved."

"Not exactly. We got the deadwood voted off the town council and we got some new, progressive people on board. I was voted mayor and also constable because I'd shot a man named Clancy Gordon who was terrorizing the town since no one wanted to confront him."

Longarm glanced sideways at Milburn. Perhaps he had underestimated the man. In fact, that now appeared to be the case. "So the town hero was elected mayor and his far-sighted thinking saved Williams from economic ruin."

"Something like that."

"Congratulations."

"Thanks. But, Marshal, I didn't tell you my story for the need of your praise or approval."

"Then why did you tell it to me?"

"For a couple of reasons. First, I want you to know that I don't back down and I can't be intimidated."

"All right. You're a brave man."

"And second, because you need to understand that this town and the offices I hold here are very important to me. Stanton Pennington has been here several times and we've talked. He's promised that, if I continue to breathe life into Williams, I may one day enjoy a much brighter and more lucrative political future."

They were almost to the train station. Longarm said, "Now that you've given me a little of your illustrious personal history, and that of the town, let me tell you something about what I stand for and where I'm going in this situation. I am convinced that Big Lips is innocent."

"She lied to you, dammit! I told you she was a master at conning people."

"I'm not easily fooled, Mayor. I've heard hundreds of stories from guilty parties and I can see through them in a moment. I think Miss Cameron is innocent and that she is resigned to going to her death as a martyr."

Milburn stopped dead in his tracks, expression incredulous. "You can't possibly be serious!"

"I am."

"Then you're a fool."

"Perhaps, but that does remain to be seen. At any rate, I'm going to go visit Governor Pennington and find out the truth. And, if it turns out that he is in any way responsible for the death of his predecessor, Governor Wilder, or Judge Maxwell Otto or anyone else, you can bet I'll bring him down."

"You in stepping into deep, deep water."

"I'm a strong swimmer. And I hope that you don't try

124

to sabotage me because it might harm your own political plans. If you did, that would be very foolish and something you would long live to regret. Do you understand me?"

"I understand that after you climb on board the train I will probably learn in the next few days that you had an unfortunate accident and were killed."

"Just don't be a part of that 'unfortunate accident'," Longarm warned. "That's all I'm asking."

"I won't be," Milburn vowed. "I wish you'd never shown up here in Arizona and I wish you'd go back to wherever it is you came from, but I won't obstruct justice or do you any wrong."

"Glad to hear that," Longarm said, as they arrived at the train depot. "But just in case you forget that pledge, I'm going into the telegraph office right now and send send a long message to my superiors in Denver. I'm going to tell them about my impressions regarding Big Lips and her innocence, about my plans to go to Prescott and interview Governor Stanton and about my discussion with you up to this moment. I'm doing this just in case I should have an 'unfortunate accident.' If that should happen, you can be sure that federal agents will soon be here in force."

"I understand."

"Good," Longarm said. "And I sure would like to find someone that knew Irene or Charlie Hanson."

"Maybe you'll find them in Prescott, seeing as that was where they supposedly had their successful freighting operation."

"Maybe."

"Marshal?"

"Yes?"

"Good luck," Milburn said, extending his hand. "I want you to know that, if Big Lips *is* innocent . . . and I'm certain she's not . . . that I'll be glad to set her free."

"Just protect her while she's locked up in that boxcar.

I understand that you have vigilantes in this town."

"All good towns have vigilantes. They are the self-cleaning mechanism of our lawless frontier."

"They are lawless mobs," Longarm countered. "And if you allow one to operate, you're unworthy to be in office."

John Milburn didn't like being told that, but he didn't say anything as they went their separate ways.

Chapter 14

Prescott was located in the inter-mountain Chino Valley and old Fort Whipple, established shortly after the Civil War, was abandoned. Upon Longarm's arrival, the picturesque town boasted almost four thousand people from all walks of life. On Montezuma Street, or Whiskey Row as some were beginning to call it, you could see gold miners, prostitutes, gamblers, loggers, cowboys and politicians. They were either rubbing shoulders in one of the more than two dozen saloons or else standing on street corners trying to generate their particular brand of income or excitement.

The moment Longarm arrived in the bustling territorial capital, he went to the modest territorial office, but was told by a young and self-important-acting aide that Stanton Pennington was in meetings all that afternoon and the next day.

"Tell the Governor that my name is Federal Marshal Custis Long and I've been sent here all the way from Denver in regards to the murder of former Governor Wilder and Judge Maxwell Otto. Tell him that I won't leave until we've talked."

"I'll pass along your message," the aide replied. "But I

doubt that it will do you any good. Maybe you should go see our own local marshal, George Butrum."

"I came to see the Governor."

"Sorry, but Governor Pennington is a very busy man."

"Well, so am I," Longarm snapped. "And my business happens to concern the fate of what I believe to be an innocent woman."

"And that person would be?"

"Lilly Cameron."

The aide snickered, making Longarm want to slap him silly.

"Just tell the governor that I won't leave until we've spoken. And add that, if he refuses to see me, I'll send a telegram to Denver advising them to contact no less than the Secretary of State in Washington, D.C. You can be sure that he'll be interested in what I am sure is a judicial breach of conduct and a legal travesty."

The aide blinked and his air of superiority disappeared. Longarm had no idea who the Secretary of State might be, but it had sounded impressive.

"Marshal, have a seat. Perhaps the Governor could spare a few minutes in order to meet with you."

"Thanks," he said, taking a chair and removing his hat.

During the next hour, Longarm observed a continual parade of aides and politicians marching down the little hallway to the governor's office. Some of them looked agitated, others confident and self-important. Longarm didn't care about any of that. What he needed to do was to discover if Governor Pennington was a man interested in truth—or a cover-up.

Finally, the aide that Longarm had first spoken to appeared and said, "The Governor will see you . . . but only for a few minutes. He is very busy these days."

"Fine," Longarm answered, allowing himself to be led up the hallway and then into an office far more impressive than he'd expected.

Stanton Pennington was tall but balding and round-faced with thick spectacles perched on a hooked beak. Longarm judged him to be in his mid-forties. When Longarm entered the man's office, Pennington was scribbling madly on a sheet of paper. He didn't even look up but went on writing until he was finished. Picking up his letter, he waved it back and forth over his desk drying the ink and then said, "Edward, see that this is posted this morning."

"Yes sir!" the aide responded, jumping forward and snatching the letter from the governor's fingers.

"Sit down, Marshal," Pennington ordered, still not looking directly at Longarm. "Did Edward inform you that I can only spare a few minutes to discuss whatever it is you came to discuss?"

"Yes, he did."

"Good!" Pennington finally looked up from his desk and studied Longarm rather like a hawk might regard a rabbit. "What is this silliness about you coming all the way from Denver to investigate the murder of my predecessor, Lance Wilder, by that murderess Big Lips Lilly Cameron?"

"I have reason to believe that they were killed by someone other than Miss Cameron."

"You have no reason to believe any such thing," Pennington said in a curt voice. "Big Lips is a murdering whore who is about to get her just reward. Marshal, if you tell me anything to the contrary, I'll tell you to get the hell out of my territory and not waste any more of the taxpayers' precious dollars."

Longarm leaned back in his chair. "Big Lips says that you or one of your minions forged the letter that is sending her to the gallows."

"Of course she did!" Pennington shouted, banging his fist on his desk top. "You ought to know that the guilty almost always try to pin the blame for their crimes on someone else. Now, does that harlot have any hard evidence against me or anyone else whose reputation is above reproach?"

Longarm chose his words carefully. "I'm not at liberty to say, Governor. My investigation is still under way."

Pennington jumped to his feet. He was clean-shaven and his loose jowls quivered with righteous indignation. He stabbed a finger across his large, cluttered desk and roared, "Your investigation is a witch hunt! I won't have anything to do with you . . . or anyone else who says that Big Lips is innocent of multiple murders."

"Does that mean," Longarm deadpanned with a straight face, "that you refuse to give her a pardon?"

"Git out of my office! Git out before I throw you out! Edward!"

The aide must have been waiting just outside the door listening to every word of their conversation because he arrived almost before the spittle from Governor Pennington's mouth hit his desk.

"Yes, sir!"

"Escort this fool out of my office and out of this building at once!"

"Yes, sir!"

Edward made the mistake of grabbing Longarm by his sleeve and trying to drag him away. Longarm batted the aide's hand aside and said, "I'll report to Washington that you were uncooperative, defensive and a damn poor excuse for a governor."

"Out! Out!"

Longarm turned on his heel and left the office. He stalked down the hallway with his heels slamming the polished wooden floor and he almost knocked the front door off its hinges.

Longarm marched back over to Whiskey Row and into the first saloon he came upon and ordered a whiskey.

"Coming right up, stranger."

When the whiskey arrived, Longarm tossed it down and ordered a second, his mind beginning to settle as his emotions regained their normal equilibrium.

"You look pretty upset about something," the bartender said. "Hope it doesn't have anything to do with me or this saloon."

"It doesn't." Longarm took a sip of the whiskey and, without really giving it any thought, asked, "What do you think of Governor Stanton Pennington?"

The bartender, an ordinary-looking man with a cleft chin wearing a clean white apron and a battered gray bowler, said, "I don't like him worth a damn. Not many people do. We all liked Lance Wilder a whole lot better, even if he was married to Big Lips."

"Well," Longarm said, his anger almost gone, "I visited Big Lips up in Williams. I think she's innocent, and did you know that they're keeping her locked in a boxcar?"

"That's what I've heard. But she won't be there much longer."

"No. She's due to hang in what . . . five days?"

"That's what those people up in Williams think . . . but don't bet on it."

Longarm's glass was almost to his face but now it froze, the whiskey forgotten. "What does that mean?" he asked, lowering his glass to the bar top.

"Well, it's not much of a secret. I thought almost everyone in Prescott knew about old Miles Ferrell and his boys going up there to spring Big Lips out of that boxcar."

"Are you serious?"

The bartender leaned closer. "The word is that Big Lips's sister is paying the Ferrell bunch five thousand dollars. They're going to bust her out of that boxcar and take her off someplace where she'll never be found."

"Big Lips has a *sister*?"

"Sure. They don't look like sisters, but they are. Dif-

131

ferent fathers, same mother, or so it's said. Both of them as bold as brass."

"Where can I find this sister?"

"Beats me. She runs a brothel here, but she's often out of town. Last I heard, she was in Denver. The truth is that Irene can't seem to stay in one place for long and Prescott seems a little too small for that woman."

Longarm tried to keep his voice calm. "You said her name was Irene?"

"Sure. Irene Cameron."

"Describe her."

Before he could do that, the bartender was called off to pour a couple of beers. Longarm had to wait several minutes while the man exchanged pleasantries with his regular customers. But finally, he came back and Longarm said, "What does Irene Cameron look like?"

"Well, she's of ordinary height. Dark brown hair and blue eyes. Pretty nicely put together, if you know what I mean."

"I know what you mean. Does she have a mole . . ." Longarm placed the tip of his forefinger on the right side of his neck, "about here?"

"Hmmm. Can't say as I remember her having a mole on her neck."

"Was she ever called Irene Hanson?"

"No. Never heard of anyone that name. But there are a lot of Irenes in Prescott. It's a popular name."

"This one was married to a man named Charlie Hanson and they owned a freight company."

"Here in Prescott?"

"That's right."

The bartender shook his head and watched a couple more customers come through the door. "Howdy boys, be right with you."

He looked at Longarm and said quickly, "I know all the businesses in town, Mister. There isn't a freighting

132

outfit or any other business owned by anyone named Hanson."

"Doesn't surprise me." Longarm drew a cigar out of his pocket and the bartender struck a match and lit it. Longarm finished his second glass of whiskey and said, "Can you tell me where this brothel is that Irene Cameron owns?"

"Sure, but I think it's still owned by her sister, Big Lips. Not that I've been there lately, you understand. I mean, I just got married a couple of months ago and I don't visit them pretty girls anymore."

"I understand. Now, where is it?"

"Go right at the door, two blocks up the street and turn right again. It's called the Pink Lady Saloon, only what men go there for isn't the whiskey which costs double and is rotgut."

"Tell me more about the Ferrell family."

The bartender glanced down at the new arrivals who looked impatient. "Look, Mister. I've got other customers waiting."

Longarm laid a dollar on the bar. "Just answer the question and then you can leave."

The bartender collected the dollar. "I don't know much else to say. The Ferrells own a cattle ranch and do well. Over the years they've either run off or bought out their neighbors. They're a tough bunch and you don't want to cross any of them or you'll be up against them all."

"Are you sure that this plot to break Big Lips out isn't just some wild rumor that someone circulated to create a stir?"

"Hey, Jimmy! We're thirsty, gawdammit! How about a couple of beers!"

"I'll be right back."

Again, Longarm had to wait but he didn't mind. What he'd just learned might be of critical importance because, if Irene Cameron was the woman on the train who called herself Irene Hanson, then the pieces of the puzzle were about to fall into place. And furthermore, this news about the Ferrell family getting ready to ride up to Williams and bust Big Lips out of the boxcar was quite a find.

When the bartender finally returned, he said, "Sorry to make you wait. How about a refill?"

"No thanks. What else can you tell me about the Ferrell family?"

"Not much, except that they're supposed to be riding up to Williams in force during the next day or two."

"Do they plan to take on the whole town of Williams?"

"That wouldn't scare them. John Milburn is the constable up there, but he's only one man and I expect he'd back down."

"But wouldn't others come to his side?"

"I doubt it. You see, Big Lips is sentenced to hang, but there are a lot of people that she befriended. By that I mean that she did a lot of good. She practically paid for our local hospital all by herself. She's given thousands of dollars to people down on their luck over the years and most of them never paid her back, but she didn't go after them or make a fuss. Big Lips has a good heart and it's a damn shame that she's going to swing."

Longarm shook his head. "I still can't imagine the Ferrells just riding up to that boxcar, tearing away the timbers and then riding off with Big Lips without firing a shot."

The bartender shrugged. "Maybe they plan to do it at night. How should I know. All I can say is they aren't to be trifled with, and I heard that Irene was paying them five thousand dollars."

"What else can you tell me about the Ferrells?"

"They live about five miles northeast of here over near the Verde River. Old Miles Ferrell was one of the first settlers in this part of the country and he picked himself a dandy place to ranch. I've been out there a couple of times and it's a real nice spread."

"How many are in the family?"

"There's four sons and a couple of daughters. But they have at least five or six cowboys on their payroll and every one of them is rough as a corn cob."

Although Longarm was low on money, the bartender had been such a fountain of potentially valuable information that he laid another dollar on the bar and said, "One last question."

"Shoot."

"I understand that the local marshal here is named George Butrum."

The bartender scoffed, leaving little doubt about what he thought about Butrum.

"Isn't he any good?"

"He's worse than worthless," the bartender spat. "Butrum is nothing but a crony of Governor Pennington and that bunch. The man is a joke in Prescott. Why are you interested in him?"

"I just decided that I'm not," Longarm said, pushing the dollar toward the man. "Thanks for your help."

"Enjoy yourself at the Pink Lady!"

Longarm had no trouble finding the Pink Lady Saloon that really wasn't a saloon. When he stepped inside, a tall woman wearing a low-cut red dress and too much paint and cheap perfume took his arm. "Hi, big man. Come to have a little party with me today?"

"I'm looking for the boss."

"Then I'm the one you want."

"I'm looking for Irene Cameron."

The woman released her grip on his arm. "Sorry, but Irene is out of town."

"When will she return?"

"I have no idea. Look, do you want a girl or what?"

"I want Irene."

The big woman studied Longarm closely. "You a friend or a customer?"

135

"A friend."

"Yeah, I knew you weren't a customer because I never forget a tall, handsome man. Come inside and buy me a drink and maybe I'll tell you something you want to know or show you something you *ought* to see."

The big woman was rough looking and she didn't have a thing that Longarm wanted to see, but he knew he had to buy her a drink if he wanted to find out anything of value.

"All right."

They walked past a garish little parlor where several younger and more attractive girls gave him big, inviting smiles. Longarm had never been one to pay for pleasures of the flesh, and he wasn't going to start now, but these women were all enticing.

"Stranger, if you see one you like, just crook your finger and I'll have her sitting on your lap before you can say hello."

"I'll keep that in mind."

"My name is Black Bertha because of my coal black hair. And, if you think the hair on my head is black then you ought to see what the rest of my hair looks like."

Black Bertha giggled obscenely and Longarm managed to dredge up an accompanying chuckle. They took a booth and, without even asking him what he liked to drink, Longarm found himself facing two icy concoctions and a burly man who stuck out his hand and grunted, "That'll cost you four dollars, Mister."

Muttering under his breath and with both of them watching him closely, Longarm drew out his wallet and counted out the money. He made sure they saw that he was nearly broke, and he sure hoped that Billy Vail had sent him some extra funds or telegraphed the local bank to advance him another hundred dollars.

"So," Black Bertha said after the bartender and bouncer had vanished, "you want to see Irene."

"That's right," Longarm said, picking up the icy drink and taking a sip. It was sweet and he set it down and reached for a cigar.

"You don't like my choice from the bar?" the woman asked, trying, but failing, to look offended.

"I'm more a beer and whiskey fella," Longarm replied.

"Bartender," she shouted loud enough to have been heard in Williams. "Bring this gentleman a damn beer!"

When it arrived, Longarm had to pay another dollar and that didn't please him one bit.

"Where is Irene?"

"Maybe in Denver, maybe in Tucson, or even San Francisco," Black Bertha said. "How should I know? She and Big Lips own this place and I just oversee things while Irene is gone."

"I really need to see her. Any way I can get in touch?"

"Afraid not." Black Bertha downed her icy drink and claimed his, saying, "You didn't have much money in that wallet. You got more someplace?"

"I might have."

"You look like a man who has some money. Good clothes and you smell decent. If you have ten dollars, I'll show you what the rest of my hair looks like."

The big woman winked and Longarm nearly jumped up and ran. Instead, he managed to say, "I really have to find Irene. It's almost a matter of life or death."

"Whose?"

"Her sister's."

Black Bertha stopped smiling. "Maybe you think that you can help Big Lips get out of that boxcar up in Williams?"

"Yeah, maybe."

"Well, we already got that one solved, stranger." She tossed down the second icy drink and rose ponderously to her feet. "Mister", she said, "I don't know and I don't care what you want with Irene, but I ain't gonna sit here

137

and listen to you anymore. If you want to pay for a woman, just snap your fingers and your wildest wish will be granted. But, if not, then you paid for that beer and you deserve to finish it before you leave. So get an eyeful of the ladies and then get your ass out of the Pink Lady."

"Why the sudden change?" Longarm asked. "I thought we were having a real nice conversation."

"You have a one track-mind and it ain't on pussy. Whatever your game is, take it someplace else."

Black Bertha turned and waddled away leaving Longarm with a sour beer and five dollars poorer.

Chapter 15

It was Longarm's standard practice to give the local law enforcement a courtesy call, but not this time. If Marshal George Butrum was as incompetent as the bartender had described, Longarm simply did not want to muddy up his own waters. Besides, he had enough to worry about without adding Butrum to the mix.

So what to do next? Well, it seemed to him that it was very possible that Irene Hanson was, in fact, Irene Cameron. That the woman he'd made love to on the train between Denver and the Raton Pass and who had been in cahoots with the bunch that robbed the train and murdered Jack Slater, was one and the same.

It made sense. Irene had probably needed the holdup money to pay the Ferrell boys to break her sister out of confinement.

If I can catch her, I might be able to solve all my problems, Longarm thought. *I can put her in prison for train robbery and I can stop this plan to spring Big Lips free from that boxcar. I might even prevent some blood-shed.*

And so, even though time was critical, Longarm elected to stay in Prescott for a day or more and see if he could capture Irene Hanson or Cameron or whatever her real name was.

"Afternoon," the clerk at the impressive, two-story Hassayampa Hotel on Gurley Street said in greeting. "How are you doing today?"

"Just fine. I need a room and I'd prefer it to be upstairs overlooking the main street."

The well-scrubbed hotel clerk opened his guest register. "I can arrange that. If you'll just sign the register, we have a nice room for only two dollars."

Longarm signed and paid the man, realizing he was down to his last few bucks. He toted his belongings upstairs and got settled in, thinking it would be nice to stretch out and take a nap after a good soak in the bathtub down at the end of the hall. But he didn't have time for those small pleasures, so he shaved and changed his clothes, then went back downstairs and headed for the telegraph office to send Billy Vail an updated report. He wouldn't, of course, tell his friend about Irene Hanson quite probably being Irene Cameron until he found the woman and confirmed the fact.

"Marshal Custis Long, eh?" the old telegraph operator asked, squinting through a pair of thick reading glasses.

"That's right."

"Could I see some identification, please?"

"Why?"

"Because we've been wired authorization for you to collect one hundred dollars at the Prescott Territorial Bank."

"In that case, I'll be happy to oblige." Longarm showed the man his badge and other identification and received the authorization which would give him some badly needed funds.

"I need to send a confidential message to Denver."

"*All* our messages are confidential."

"Sure." Longarm spelled out a message to Billy Vail

explaining what he had learned from the editor in Flagstaff as well as from Governor Pennington. He ended by writing, HAVE HIGH HOPES TO WRAP THIS UP SOON. BELIEVE BIG LIPS CAMERON ABOUT TO BE FREED. WILL KEEP YOU POSTED.

"You think that woman is going to be freed?" the telegraph operator asked in a low and confidential tone of voice.

"That's our little secret. I thought everyone in town knew that Irene Cameron had paid the Ferrells five thousand dollars to spring her sister, Big Lips."

"I didn't know that and I know about everything that goes on in this town," the man said.

"Well, it was probably just a false rumor," Longarm told the man. "But anyway, please keep it to yourself."

"I hope Irene does manage to free Big Lips. I never did believe she killed Governor Wilder or Judge Otto. I've known Lilly and her kid sister since they were both just little sprouts. And while I'd be the first to admit they were a couple of hellions, neither one of them would murder in cold blood."

"What about those two men that Big Lips killed in a fight?"

"Self-defense! How could you blame someone who was trying to save their own life?"

"Well, I couldn't. But what about Irene?"

"She's actually tougher than Lilly."

Longarm was more than a little interested in this assessment. "How so?"

"Well, she just is," the telegraph operator who wore a name badge identifying him as *Ralph* said. "Lilly is a few years older, but Irene was always the one that was scheming to get her way. Funny that Lilly turned out to be the one who made all the money while Irene has always just sort of gotten by."

"Was Irene married to a guy named Charlie Hanson?"

"Nope. His name was Charlie Bell. He was a mule-skinner and hard drinker. Got stabbed a week ago going home from the saloon. No one misses him. Charlie Bell was a real troublemaker and there was many the time that I saw Irene with a shiner or fat lip he'd given her when he was drunk. Of course, she gave him the same and sometimes even better. Oh, Irene is a tough one, all right. I sure wouldn't want to be her enemy."

And she's a train robber, Longarm thought, keeping that part of it to himself.

Longarm went to the bank and got his much-needed cash. Then he headed back in the direction of the Pink Lady Saloon and found a shady place where it was not likely he'd be observed. He sat down, leaned back against a building, lit a cigar and figured to spend a while watching the brothel in hopes of spotting Irene. He'd give it the rest of the day and evening and maybe even part of the night. If he didn't see her by tomorrow, maybe she was out of town.

Doing surveillance was one of the worst parts of being a lawman, but Longarm knew it was a crucial part of his work. There was a time to act and a time to sit and watch, and sometimes the latter reaped the greater returns.

He sat and smoked two cigars watching the customers go in and out of the Pink Lady until darkness fell. Then, unable to control the rumblings in his stomach, Longarm went and had a quick dinner before hurrying back to take up his watch. One thing he did learn was that the Pink Lady and Black Bertha were kept mighty busy. Why, he must have counted fifty men that came and went, almost always with big smiles on their faces.

Thinking about women got him thinking about the great lovemaking he'd shared with Irene on the train. It was a damned pity that she turned out to be such a big liar who was tied up with murder and robbery. No doubt she'd not been a part of the actual murder itself, but that didn't matter. If she was part of the plan, she'd be charged with murder and probably sent to prison for a long, long time. What a shame and what a waste.

Longarm was yawning and thinking he ought to give up the watch and go get some sleep in his hotel bed. After all, he'd paid two dollars and he ought to get some benefit for his . . . no, the *government's* money.

But then he saw her. Irene!

It was dark and he couldn't see Irene's lovely face but he knew her walk and figure oh so well. Instantly awake, Longarm was stiff with the cold and slow to come to his feet. He pitched his cigar aside and started across the street. Then he heard something behind him and his hand went for his gun.

Too late. The next thing he knew, a light exploded behind his eyes and he felt himself falling.

Chapter 16

When Longarm awoke the next day, it was to find himself tied, bound and gagged in a chicken house. Chickens were sitting on roosts overhead and he was covered with their droppings.

Damn!

Longarm swore into his gag and struggled to sit up, but his legs and arms were not only tied behind his back, but cleverly roped to some of the cross beams of the chicken house so that it was impossible to do much more than squirm.

Damn!

He snarled and bit the gag but that didn't do a bit of good except to send the hens into a squawking dither. When Longarm flopped around, the hens panicked and went flying out into the outer chicken pen, leaving more of their disgusting droppings on his person.

Longarm relaxed and closed his eyes. It was very dim in the chicken house and it didn't smell good either. He could hear the chickens giving him hell, but paid them no mind.

What a revolting predicament! Who had sneaked up behind him last night and cracked his head?

Longarm's head was definitely cracked. It hurt like blazes, and when he shook it, he felt as if his brains had leaked out into the malodorous mixture of straw, feathers, dirt and chicken shit upon which he lay.

Why hadn't he been killed? Why just bound and gagged and left in this despicable hen house? It must have been Black Bertha or the telegraph operator who had alerted someone of his interest in Irene. Or maybe it was even Irene who had seen him and decided to have him taken out of commission.

Longarm heaved a deep, troubled sigh. None of it made any sense and that wasn't going to change until he managed to get free. Hell, he didn't even know if he was still in town or if someone had taken him to a ranch or farm. Why, he might be miles from Prescott and at the mercy of some chicken-loving murderer.

Longarm struggled mightily but it did no good. Whoever had tied him up knew some real tricks of the trade. The trouble was that with his arms and legs pulled up behind him as far as they could go, he could barely move. And yet, he *had* to move. Had to get free because his life probably depended upon it, and maybe Big Lips Lilly Cameron's life as well.

The afternoon lasted forever. Longarm struggled until his wrists burned and he knew they were bloody. He kicked and squirmed and fought his bonds with all his strength. He told himself that if he ever got free of this mess, he was going to find out who was behind this trouble and he was going to throttle them with his bare hands.

The sun began to go down. Longarm knew that because he saw its red streaks though the cracks in the hen house walls. He knew it because the hens and a big red rooster moved cautiously back into the hen house and took to the roost over his head. They began to shit on him again as they complained loudly of his presence. The whole experience was disgusting and humiliating.

145

Darkness came and his head was throbbing and his throat was as dry as the chicken house floor.

Finally he heard the squeak of a gate being opened and then he heard her voice. "Marshal Custis Long. My, my. What a fix you have placed us all in."

He twisted his head around and there, back-dropped by the chicken house door and the fading light was Irene. Longarm expelled a muffled curse and thrashed around as she watched. He could not see her face in the shadows and that was probably just as well because he knew she would not be looking at him with tender, sympathetic eyes.

"Custis, I'm sorry for your misery but I really had no alternative but to have you brought here in this pathetic condition. And now, while the Ferrell men go to free my sister, I have to decide what is to be done with you. If I let you loose, you'll send me to prison and my sister back to the gallows."

She shook her head. "I'm afraid that I have no choice but to silence you . . . forever."

Longarm quit struggling. He couldn't tell because of the poor light, but he figured that Irene had a gun in her hand and she was about to kill him. After all, she was right. If he survived, she'd go to prison for the rest of his natural life.

"You know, I was so sorry that you showed up in Flagstaff asking questions about me and my sister. And then you saw her in Williams and she said that you seemed like a good man. I told her that you were, indeed, very good . . . especially in bed. What a pity that it had to end this way."

Longarm couldn't help but grunt and cuss some more. Besides, it took his mind off the bullet that was probably about to enter his body and end this misery.

"Custis, I have a confession to make."

Longarm heard Irene sigh. He could visualize her face

as she stood near him playing the role of executioner.

"I killed Governor Lance Wilder. He was messing around with every whore in town while being married to Lilly. He even propositioned me! He was no good and I guess that leaves just one loose thread. Who killed Judge Otto? Well, I'm not going to tell you except that it wasn't me. Nope. I thought about it, but I didn't do it. I know who killed the judge and it wasn't my sister."

Irene giggled. "I love a mystery. I think I'll leave you with that one before you die."

Longarm steeled himself for the bullet.

"But before I kill you, we're going to share a cigar and a bottle of whiskey. Not that I'm going to untie your hands or your legs . . . no, that would be very stupid. But I will remove the gag and help you smoke and drink. And I'll try and drag you out of this damned stinking hen house. Why would I do such nice things? Because I'm sorry it has to come to this. You were a wonderful lover and traveling companion."

Longarm heard the chicken pen gate squeak in protest again and figured the woman had gone off to get some whiskey and cigars. He struggled with all his might, but the result was just the same as it had been before. No give and no release. He was doomed. It was clear to him now that Irene whatever her last name was had, indeed, killed the former governor. The woman was demented. She might even have gotten the naive Jack Slater to lower his guard and then slashed his throat, mocking his weakness.

I've got to figure out something when this madwoman comes back or I'm finished, Longarm thought, his mind whirling. *I've got to get untied and stop her before she kills me!*

It seemed like a long time passed before Irene returned with a lantern and a sack which he assumed contained a bottle of whiskey. The woman set the lantern down close beside him and said, "I'm not going to untie your hands or legs but I do think I'm going to have to untie these ropes that go up to the rafters. Pretty good job, huh?"

Longarm couldn't answer, but it sure felt good when she cut the ropes that had strained his limbs upward until they ached. Now he rolled over onto his back and lay still, every thought focused on how to somehow over-power this crazy, cunning woman.

She smiled down at him. "I'm going to drag you out of here so we can sit in the moonlight and enjoy the night sky. There's a horse watering trough not very far from here, and that's where I'm going to wash your face and comb your hair. Unfortunately, there's nothing I can do about the way that you smell. Oh, I might be able to get you into the horse trough but then you'd nearly freeze and not be able to enjoy your last minutes of life."

Longarm wasn't sure that Irene had the strength to drag him through the manure and out of the chicken pen, but he knew that he would have more room to maneuver, so he did everything possible to help.

"You're heavy," she grunted, as they struggled out of the hen house and across the pen, "but I already knew that. I knew that old Miles Ferrell wouldn't go along with murdering you, so I had no choice but to hide you where you'd never be found by him or his boys."

That told Longarm he was at the Ferrell Ranch and the old man and his sons weren't in on the plan to have him murdered. Good. If he could somehow overwhelm Irene, then they would not be yet another monumental obstacle to overcome.

Irene was grunting and puffing by the time they crawled, crabbed and scrabbled over to the horse trough. She propped Longarm up against the water trough and went back to retrieve the whiskey in the hen house. During those few moments of her absence, Longarm's bound hands explored the corner of the horse trough until he found a loose nail. He pried it loose and then began to frantically work it into the knot that bound his wrists.

"All right then," Irene said, returning to sit cross-legged in the dirt beside him. "There's a full moon out tonight and isn't this romantic?"

She's crazy as a loon. Why didn't I see a hint of it on the train? Was I totally blinded by her talented and passionate lovemaking?

"Custis," she mused, gazing up at the moon, "if I could figure out a way without you taking advantage of me, I'd make love to you just one last time."

Irene chuckled and the sound of it sent a chill all the way up and down Longarm's spine.

"All right," she said, dragging a revolver out of the sack and then a bottle of whiskey, two glasses and two cigars. "Here's the ground rules that you must obey or I'll end our party on a very sour note."

He waited, hearing his heart hammer in his chest.

Irene continued, "First, I am going to remove that gag. If you curse at me or say anything mean or threatening, I'll shoot you. Is that understood? I hope you understand because I mean what I say. You saved my life in Denver from those thugs. You were wonderful to me on the train and this is the way I mean to repay your kindnesses. But I *will* shoot you if you become angry or start saying cruel things. Nod your head if you understand and agree to be a gentleman like you were on the train."

Longarm vigorously nodded his head.

"Good. I knew you'd be sensible and appreciate the gesture I'm making for old times' sakes." She leaned forward and removed the hated gag. Longarm sucked in a couple of deep breaths and fought down his first impulse which was to call her a lunatic.

"Isn't that much better?"

Longarm began to work the nail deeper into the hard knot that bound his wrists. Working it blind, he couldn't really tell yet if he was actually freeing his hands, but it was his only chance and he meant to keep trying. With his hands bound behind his back, Irene couldn't see how hard he was trying.

"Much better," he managed to say.

"I'm sorry about having to hide you in the chicken house but, like I explained, I had no choice. Miles Ferrell is a hard man but he wouldn't have gone along with killing a federal lawman."

"I understand."

Lilly extracted a wash cloth and bar of soap from the sack. She dunked the wash cloth in the water trough, then palmed some soap into it and gently began to clean his face. "How is your head feeling?"

"It hurts. I was watching you from across the street so I know you must have had some help. Who hit me?"

"That's my secret. Now just be quiet while I dry your face and comb your hair. You have nice hair, Custis. You've got nice *everything*."

"I'm glad you remember."

"Oh, I do! If I didn't, you'd be dead."

"So you're the one that killed Wilder and Judge Otto."

"Only Lance Wilder," she said. "Don't try and be clever and trick me because I don't like that."

"All right." Longarm knew that he would have to tread very lightly or he'd set Irene off and she would fill him full of holes. "What now?"

"Now I am going to comb your hair and then we'll enjoy our whiskey and cigars."

"Do you smoke cigars?"

"Sure."

"You didn't on the train."

"Of course not." Irene giggled. "How would it have appeared? But out here . . . well, who cares? No one is going to see what we do."

"Are we going to do anything besides drink and smoke?"

"I told you I'd like us to make love but I know you can't be trusted that much."

"Yes, I can! I could make love to you and still keep my hands tied behind me."

"I doubt that."

"Pour us some whiskey and we can talk about it."

Irene poured them two glasses and confessed, "I found this bottle in the ranch house. The old man keeps a private reserve of his best. He'll probably discover the theft, but since I'm paying him five thousand dollars to free my sister from those people up in Williams, what does a mere bottle of whiskey matter. Right?"

"Right."

"Are your wrists all bloody from trying to wiggle out of my knots? I can't see them."

"It doesn't matter."

"I don't want you to suffer. I could have had you killed right after you fell into our hands, but I wanted some time to tell you how sorry I am that it had to end up this way."

"You don't *have* to kill me, Irene."

"I do if I want to save myself from a noose."

"What if I promised you I'd try and get you a lesser sentence?"

She laughed coldly. "You mean maybe only twenty or thirty years in the Yuma Prison? No thanks. I visited my sister there once and I knew that I'd rather die and go burn in hell than wind up in prison. Lilly feels the same way."

Longarm was willing to say whatever it took to save his life. "What if I just let you go free?"

"Oh, but you wouldn't! I questioned you on the train quite closely about how you feel about the law and your sworn oath. And you told me that you never made exceptions. No, Custis, you'd send me to the gallows or to prison, so please don't lie to me anymore or I will get angry and kill you before we've had our little farewell party."

"So that's what this is?"

"Of course." She filled their glasses and raised her own to her lips. "To love and to lovemaking!"

He dipped his chin in silent agreement, fingers working madly with the unseen nail and knot behind his back.

"Now your turn," she said, placing the glass to his lips. "Drink up, Custis. It'll make the pain of parting much easier."

Longarm did as he was told and she had been right— old man Ferrell's whiskey was prime. Just as importantly, the bottle was large and nearly full. That meant that Irene might get drunk enough to give him an edge . . . as long as he didn't get drunk, too.

"Now the cigars," she said, lighting one and puffing it solemnly. "Not bad. Also compliments of Miles Ferrell. He's a real skinflint except for his own precious extravagances. And to think that I almost married one of his boys. That's when I got to really know the old man."

"Don't you like him?"

"He's okay, but one of those that knows everything. And he's boring. He loves nothing better than to go on and on about how he pioneered in this valley and overcame all kinds of dangers to build his ranching empire. You hear his story the first time and you think that he did do a hell of a lot. But after you've heard the story six or seven times and the facts change with each telling, you just know that the old man is full of crap. That he was more lucky than brave or daring."

"Yeah, I guess that's a big part of success. Is that what your sister and Wilder were . . . lucky?"

"I don't want to talk about Lilly," she said, expression turning somber in the bright mountain moonlight. "Or about the great Governor Wilder. You should have seen him before I killed the slug . . . he begged and cried and

152

moaned. Oh how he carried on for his worthless, cheating life! I didn't waver, though. I killed him and it's a fact that I'm proud of. I think he would have had my sister killed if he'd lived. He was ashamed of her . . . and me by association."

Longarm was so fascinated by these revelations that he kept forgetting to work the nail at his wrist bonds. And it seemed, although he couldn't tell for sure, that they were loosening. Anyway, it was important to keep Irene talking.

"So what happened between you and the Ferrell fella?"

"Oh, he wanted to marry me real bad and I probably should have gone through with it, but I lost my temper and told the old man he was a bore and a braggart. That sort of soured things and I guess he talked Billy out of marrying me. He probably threatened to disinherit him if we were wed."

"I see."

Irene gazed up at the moon and puffed contentedly on her cigar. Then she passed it to Longarm saying, "It is kinda cold but beautiful out tonight. Don't you agree?"

"I sure do."

She stared at him and giggled.

"What's so funny?"

"Your clothes are covered with chicken shit. You really are a pathetic sight."

"I suppose so."

She emptied her glass and poured another. Irene took a long, shuddering gulp, then poured some more down his throat. It sure was smooth, but Longarm wasn't in the proper frame of mind to enjoy it.

"When are they breaking your sister out of that box-car?"

"They might be doing it right now, although I expect they'll wait until the town is asleep. Sometime well after midnight."

"Will they bring her back here?"

"No."

"Where. . . ."

Irene blew a cloud of smoke in his face and wagged her finger in front of his eyes. "I don't want to talk about her. Remember?"

Longarm heard the chilling edge to her voice. "Sorry. I forgot."

"That's all right. Just don't forget again."

"I won't."

"I'll bet you're starving."

"I am hungry."

"There's some fried chicken left over in the kitchen. I could get you some and help you eat it but then . . . maybe you're sick of anything to do with chickens."

He would eat dung if it would buy him more time to work on the bonds that bound his wrists behind his back. "I'd still like to eat."

"I'd go inside and get a couple of drumsticks, but I don't trust you alone out here. So let's forget about food and enjoy our cigars and this bottle of whiskey."

"Fine with me. Are you going to shoot me when the whiskey is all gone?"

"I have to!" Irene's admission came out almost in a sob. "Don't you understand that I couldn't bear to go to prison and I don't want to be hanged?"

"I understand. And I'm sorry for that train guard whose throat was slashed. His name was Jack Slater, and he left a mother who needed him down in Santa Fe."

"That wasn't my fault. Those boys were just supposed to knock him in the head, but they were crazy mean. I'm glad you killed all three. It gave me a lot more to spend."

"Yeah," Longarm said. "I'll bet it did. What are you going to do with all that money and gold?"

"Well, I had to pay the Ferrells five thousand to spring my sister from that boxcar."

154

"That still leaves a lot."

"Enough to take us far, far away."

"Where to?"

She looked closely at him. "You're just full of questions. Custis, you never give up trying to be a lawman, do you?"

"I guess it's a habit."

"Well, I don't think it matters if I tell you. Can't hurt when you're dead can it?"

"Nope."

"We're going to live in Reno."

"That's nice country."

"Yes it is. Lilly has never been there, but I have. I've long wanted to return. We'll do that very soon and have enough money to do whatever we wish."

"Maybe Big Lips will want to start up another brothel."

"We're going to become ladies. We'll come up with a whole new identity. Names, backgrounds. Everything."

"Clever."

"As you well know, it's done all the time out in the West."

"That's right."

Irene took another drink and then smoked for a few minutes in silence before saying, "I sure am going to hate to kill you, Custis."

"I'm going to hate it even more."

"Wish there was another way. If you weren't so dedicated to the law I'd take a chance on you."

"I could change."

"Not before you sent me to my doom." She pressed the bottle to his lips and ordered with a touch of urgency in her voice, "Drink up. Drink plenty!"

Longarm took two long swallows and then worked the nail until he felt for sure that the knots were coming untied from around his wrists. Just a few more minutes and he'd hopefully have it.

"I'm getting tired of talking," Irene said. "I wish we could make love."

"Start unbuttoning buttons and let's see what happens," he suggested.

A smile came slowly to her full lips. "Do you really think you could?"

"Why not?"

"Well, I just thought that, since you were about to die it would be hard to get excited about lovemaking."

"If I have to die, why not do it one last time?"

Irene licked her lips and rubbed her breasts. She took a long series of gulps on the bottle. "Yeah," she breathed. "Why not?"

"Give me another drink," he said, knowing he wasn't prepared for what he was about to be asked. But this time, it was do . . . or die.

Irene gave him a drink and then she put the bottle and her cigar aside and began to unbutton his pants. "You better be up to this," she warned, picking up the gun.

Longarm worked frantically on the knot behind his back, but it wasn't coming as quickly as he'd expected. He took a sharp breath when Irene tore his manhood out of his pants.

"It's still limp," she said, accusation thick in her voice.

"I . . . I'm sorry. Why don't you give it a little encouragement? You know. Like you did while we traveled on the train?"

"All right."

Irene bent over and took him in her mouth. While her lips worked on his rod, Longarm worked hard with the nail and the knot.

"Now you're getting there," she cooed, looking up.

"Really?"

"Sure. Can't you tell?"

Longarm realized that he was stiffening and that was

quite a surprise, given the seriousness of the circumstances.

"Come on," she urged, her lips moving up and down his stiffening member. "You can do it!"

To his utter amazement, she was right. And the next thing he knew, Irene was hiking up her dress and pulling off her underpants. "Stretch out a little more," she ordered.

Longarm stretched, still working the knot behind his back. Then Irene straddled his body and eased down on his manhood. Without any of the usual preliminaries, she began to move her bottom up and down, making it hard for him to concentrate on getting his hands free.

"Oh boy," she moaned, throwing her head back and gazing up at the moon. "I didn't think we'd be able to do this. You're one hell of a man, Custis!"

When Irene started to bounce up and down, Longarm couldn't do a thing with the knot. So he closed his eyes and let it happen until they were both howling up at the moon and slamming together in ecstasy.

Irene rolled off him and lay panting, long, lovely bare legs golden in the moonlight. Longarm tore at his wrists and the knot until his hands suddenly came free. Then, while she was still floating on a sea of pleasure and unprepared, he rolled sideways, hands flying for the gun resting at her side.

Irene screamed and grabbed her weapon. They rolled, with Longarm trying desperately to will feeling into his circulation-deadened fingers. The Colt exploded between them and Longarm felt as if he'd been hit with a red hot branding iron . . . but it was Irene who cried out and went limp.

"Dammit!" he shouted, ankles still tied. "Irene!"

The bullet had entered just under her ribs and it must have traveled up into her torso because crimson bubbles formed on her lips.

"Irene, I didn't mean to kill you," Longarm said, cradling her head to his chest.

"It's all right, lover. Don't feel bad because I really was going to kill you."

"Who murdered Judge Maxwell?"

Her lips moved but the words were so soft Longarm couldn't hear them plainly. Leaning closer, he repeated his question. "If your sister didn't kill the judge, then who did?"

She was trying hard to tell him but ran out of time. Longarm felt her shudder in his arms and he heard her ominous death rattle.

Then, Irene was gone.

Chapter 17

Longarm carried Irene's body into the ranch house and laid her out on the big dining room table. He cleaned her up just as she'd done for him and then he took a bath, shaved and found clean clothes in one of the bedrooms. Taking a quick tour around the ranch yard, he located a buckboard still hitched to a pair of horses.

Stuffed under an old tarp lying in its bed was a tied packet of fresh one hundred dollar bills. It didn't take much guesswork for Longarm to figure that this was part of the money that had been stolen up on Raton Pass. He took the cash back into the ranch house for counting and learned that there was exactly five thousand dollars.

The payment to Miles Ferrell and his sons for springing Big Lips from that boxcar turned jail, he thought. *I wonder where Irene hid the four sacks of gold and the other twenty five thousand? Maybe whoever hit me over the head down in Prescott then helped her load me into that buckboard has the money. If I can find Irene's accomplice, I've about got this case solved.*

Longarm wasn't exactly sure what to do next, but his head ached fiercely and he was so worn down that he stretched out on a huge cowhide couch. He intended to rest a few minutes, but instead fell sleep and he didn't awaken until late the next morning when he heard the sound of horses galloping into the ranch yard.

Longarm rolled off the couch and grabbed his six-gun. Wiping sleep from his eyes and shaking the cobwebs from his mind, he went over to stand next the the dining room table beside Irene's body, which was now stiff with rigor mortis.

"Sorry it had to work out that way," he told the corpse. "But you said you'd rather die than go to prison and that's what you deserved even if Jack Slater's death was a surprise."

When the front door banged opened, a rough looking man in his sixties with bushy white eyebrows and mustache to match bulled inside followed by three or four men that Longarm assumed were his sons. They were all wearing boots, spurs and chaps and there was a heaviness in their stride that told him they'd spent a long night in the saddle. It was dim inside the house and they didn't see Longarm until they were almost face to face.

"What the . . ."

"Hold it!" Longarm warned. "I'm a United States Marshal and you're all under arrest!"

When one of the younger men started to reach for the gun on his hip, Longarm emptied a round into the ceiling. "Don't move or you're a dead man!"

They all froze.

"Mr. Ferrell, if anyone makes the mistake of going for their gun, you're going to be the first one to die."

"Steady boys," the old patriarch warned. "Mister, is that Irene Cameron?"

"Yes."

"Did you kill her?"

"I had no choice. She was going to kill me."

"How do I know you aren't just some crazy bastard that will try and kill all of us?"

Longarm showed them his badge. "Like I said, I'm a federal marshal. Now all of you raise your hands over your head and back out the door real slow."

"Pa, we don't . . ."

"Do as he says!" Miles Ferrell snapped.

Longarm backed them out of the house into the ranch yard. There were other cowboys outside and when they saw their boss being held at gunpoint, they acted like they were going to get stupid, so Longarm repeated his warning.

"Everyone line up and keep your hands over your heads!"

"What the hell is the meaning of this!" Ferrell swore. "This is my home!"

"You just freed Big Lips from that boxcar up in Williams, didn't you?"

The old man glared at Longarm. "That's right, but she is innocent."

"Maybe so," Longarm told the man. "But you've still broken the law. Was anyone hurt up there?"

Ferrell shook his head. "But I think someone's about to get hurt here pretty quick."

"It doesn't have to be that way," Longarm said.

"Are we under arrest?"

Longarm had been asking himself the very same question. If he put the old man, his sons and the hired hands under arrest, it was going to be hard to deliver them all to jail. And no doubt Miles Ferrell was very influential in Prescott and the whole bunch would quickly be freed.

"Well!" Ferrell demanded.

"Maybe not," Longarm hedged. "I think you and me ought to go inside and have a long talk."

"Pa, don't do it! He killed Irene and he'll probably kill you."

"No I won't," Longarm said. "If I did that, what would my chances be of getting out of your house alive?"

"Zero," the cowboy growled. "You wouldn't live two more minutes."

"Then I'd have to be crazy to kill your father and I'm not crazy."

"You're wearing my damn shirt and pants!" another of the rancher's sons blurted. "Pa, maybe he's just a thief and Irene caught him going through the house and he killed her."

"He had a badge."

"But he might have killed a marshal and took it off his body. Or he might just have stole it from a lawman."

Ferrell nodded. "My son has a good point."

"I was sent here from Denver to investigate the murder of Governor Lance Wilder and Maxwell Otto, a federal judge. I've got a telegram and some other papers to prove that, but we'll look at them inside and then talk."

Ferrell turned to his sons and ranch hands. "Since he's got the drop on us, I'm going to go inside. You boys wait out by the barn. If there's trouble, you'll know about it soon enough."

One of the sons, a tall, rangy man with a red beard and hard blue eyes said, "Mister, if you hurt or kill my father we'll take you alive and kill you slow."

"I appreciate the warning," Longarm said, backing into the house with his gun still trained on the old rancher. "But it wasn't necessary."

Once inside the house, Longarm shut and locked the front door. "Go sit down."

"Show me those papers first."

Longarm had a telegram from Billy Vail and he unfolded it. "This ought to satisfy you."

Ferrell read the telegram and then handed it back. "So what happens next, Marshal?"

"Let's sit down and see if we can come up with a solution to our problems."

"I don't have a problem," Ferrell said.

"You agreed to accept five thousand dollars in return for freeing Big Lips Cameron from jail and a hanging. That's a pretty serious crime. Serious enough to send all of you to prison."

"Lilly Cameron is innocent of murdering either Wilder or Otto. She was framed by Governor Stanton Pennington."

"Any proof of that?"

The rancher shook his head. "And that's why we took the law into our own hands. It would have been a stain on the whole territory if we'd allowed the woman to hang."

"But you didn't do it for entirely honorable reasons," Longarm pointed out. "You did it for cash."

"Yeah. Sure. Cattle prices are down and the last couple of summers have been dry. I've taken some big losses and needed the money. I mean to hang onto this spread and hand it down to my sons. It's their birthright."

"You took money to break the law. But for what it's worth, Irene confessed that she was the one that killed Wilder."

"She told you that?"

Longarm nodded his head. "That's right. But before she died, she also said that she did not kill Judge Maxwell Otto. I think that she was trying to tell me the real murderer as she died."

"How come you had to kill her?" the rancher demanded.

"She had a gun and was going to shoot me. Irene was part of a train holdup where she used three other men to rob a safe. During the robbery, the security guard was murdered. Irene knew she was going to prison or the gallows. I think she preferred death, although the gun went off accidentally."

"Are you sure of that?"

"No," Longarm admitted. "She might have pulled the

trigger on purpose to take her own life. It was dark and happened fast. I doubt I'll ever be sure why the gun went off and it happened to be pointed at that instant in her direction."

"I thought that she'd also killed Judge Otto. He was no good and on Pennington's payroll. But, if Irene didn't kill the judge, who did?"

"That," Longarm said, "is what I have to find out. When I was struck from behind across from the Pink Lady Saloon, Irene must have had an accomplice. Maybe he was the one that killed the judge."

"But you don't know who that could have been?"

"No." Longarm frowned. "One of your sons was to marry Irene. Was he with you last night?"

"Sure. Were you thinking that Paul might have murdered Judge Otto!"

"Easy," Longarm said. "If Paul was with you then he couldn't have been the one that crept up behind me last evening, cracked my skull and pitched me into that buckboard outside."

Ferrell heaved a deep sigh. "Look," he said, "it's been a long, tough night and I'm beat. Furthermore, I'm in no mood for mysteries or riddles, so why don't you put that gun away and get off my ranch."

"Where is Big Lips now?"

Ferrell's lips drew down at the corners and he shook his head. "Even though I'm not getting paid, I'm still not telling you where we took her this morning."

"Listen," Longarm told the man, his voice hardening. "Until I find out who *really* killed the judge, Big Lips is still considered his murderer. In order to clear her of all charges so that she can live without worrying for the rest of her days about being caught . . . I have to figure out who really did kill Judge Otto."

"Then do it."

"I can't without help, and Big Lips is the logical choice

to point me in the right direction. With Irene dead and Big Lips missing, I hold an empty hand."

"What are you asking me to do?"

"Take me to Big Lips."

Ferrell turned and walked over to Irene's body. He shook his head. "Did she really admit to killing Lance Wilder?"

"She did."

"Well, good for her. Irene was wild, headstrong and kind of crazy. I knew she'd twist my son around her little finger and get him into deep trouble. She was beautiful, but badly flawed."

"Where's Big Lips right now?"

"Oh hell, I'll take you to her," the rancher said after a few minutes. "She's not too far away. We couldn't bring her here to the ranch because we figured that Mayor Milburn would form a posse and track us. There just wasn't any way that we could hide the trail of a dozen horses."

"What shall we do with Irene's body?"

"We'll bury her here. There's a little cemetery in Prescott but she never liked it there much. She was always talking about going back to Reno. To bad she didn't make it. I'll have Paul and a couple of the boys dig her grave and carve her a marker. Maybe even read a couple passages from the Good Book."

"That would be nice." Longarm didn't see any point in telling the rancher about his having made love to Irene both on the train and during the last few crazy minutes of her life. "What about a casket?"

Ferrell thought about that for a minute. "I'll ask the boys to get some lumber and fix up a pine box. When Lilly finds out about this, she's going to be awful upset."

"Perhaps it would be best to wait for her to come before we lay her sister in the ground."

"I guess it would," Ferrell said. "But we can't forget about them boys from Williams. Mayor Milburn is ambitious. If he thinks he can gain some points with Governor Pennington, you can bet he'll try."

"Milburn is only a part-time constable in Williams. He's out of his jurisdiction. If he and a posse arrive, I'll handle them."

Ferrell's eyes flashed with anger. "If you don't, me and my boys will. Milburn and his bunch were practically frothing at the bit waiting to see Lilly hang. Why, there was a lot of talk up there about charging a dollar admission! And you know what? They'd be the first ones to tell you they were all Christians."

"They're no longer in charge," Longarm vowed. "No matter what, Big Lips isn't going back to that boxcar and I'm not about to let those people lynch her at their gallows or off the limb of a big tree."

"Glad to hear that, but that bunch will be loaded for bear. And just in case lead starts flying, me and my boys will be ready to back you up." The old man put his hat back on and started for the door. "Let's go see Big Lips Lilly."

They went outside and Longarm stood off a short distance while the rancher ordered a casket to be made and then explained what he'd agreed to do. He ended by saying, "The Marshal has me convinced that, for Lilly to ever live in peace, he has to prove that she didn't kill Judge Maxwell Otto. So we're going to find her and see if we can get to the bottom of it."

"Well, who killed Wilder?" one of the sons asked.

"Irene," the old man answered. "It was Irene that killed the governor."

"No!"

"Listen Paul. I know you loved her but even you told me she sometimes got real crazy. The way I see it, Irene did us a favor by killing Wilder. We all know he was a cheat and a liar. That he'd sell out his best friend for a dollar."

166

"Sure, Pa, but . . ."

"Son, you have to put her behind you. She's dead and all we can do now is just give her a decent Christian burial."

There were tears streaming down the young man's face and Longarm sure wished that things had turned out better but, given Irene's confession, that had been impossible.

"Let's take the buckboard," Ferrell growled. "My butt is already saddle sore. I'm not used to covering so many miles on horseback anymore. But when I was your age, I once rode all the way from Prescott to Ehrenberg on the Colorado River and back in five days just for the hell of it. I was as tough as a boot and hell bent for leather."

Longarm got into the buckboard and they drove off.

"I was wondering," Ferrell said, "whatever happened to that railroad money you said Irene helped steal?"

"I've got part of it on me. I don't know where the rest is. That's something that I'll have to find out. My guess is that whoever hit me in the back of the head has it."

"She had some rough friends in Prescott."

Longarm glanced sideways with sudden interest. "Anyone in particular?"

"No."

"Too bad. Until I get to the bottom of this, Big Lips Lilly is still facing a murder conviction."

"But you said you believed she was innocent."

"I do, but I have to prove it," Longarm replied. "Which direction are we going?"

"East into the mountains. Just follow those fresh tracks we made coming down from the northeast."

Longarm drove the buckboard across the valley. He sure hoped that Big Lips hadn't decided to go on the run, because he was tired of this chase and anxious to get everything wrapped up so that he could make a report to Billy Vail. Once things were cleared up, he might even decide to head south into the desert for a short vacation.

He liked Tucson just fine at this time of the year. Not that things were tough right here. Why, the sun was shining and although there was snow on the mountain peaks surrounding Chino Valley, the air was surprisingly warm. It felt like spring, even though that was still a couple months away.

Ferrell had lapsed into a brooding silence. "Miles, do you like this country?"

"You bet. Northern Arizona is the best country I've ever found. We're a little short up here on water, but I got all I need for my cattle. This valley has good climate and good grass. What else could a man think who came here broke and now owns a fine ranch?"

"It's sure a lot warmer here than Denver at this time of year."

Ferrell snorted. "I been to Denver and nearly froze to death in the winter of seventy-nine. Blizzard hit and I was driving mules out on the plains east of town. The wind sure did howl and, if I hadn't gotten lucky and found a homestead, I'd have been a goner and so would my mules."

"Does the snow get very deep in this valley?"

"Nope. It usually melts in a day or two." Ferrell dragged a plug of chewing tobacco out of his pocket and gnawed off a chunk. After chewing it for a few minutes to get it soft, he added, "Winters here are easy, but it can get pretty deep up in Williams and Flagstaff 'cause they're a few thousand feet higher."

"I see." Longarm drove along for a while and then said, "Do you really expect John Milburn to come after you with a posse?"

"Yep. I've had a run-in or two with the man. He don't like me and I don't like him. It'll be personal and don't be fooled by his looks . . . Milburn can handle a gun and he can fight."

"I figured as much."

"Before he became a mayor, he was a blacksmith and then a gunsmith. He knows weapons and is a crack shot. He's never lost a shooting match."

"Thanks for the warning, but I can't imagine he'd be stupid enough to want to take on all of us."

"Oh, I doubt very much he'd do that either," the rancher agreed. "But if he comes upon us and Lilly before we get back to the ranch . . . and there's ten or fifteen guns to our pair . . . well, that's another matter."

"Yeah. I see what you mean. How much farther to where Big Lips is hidden?"

"About four miles up that box canyon and into those trees."

Longarm followed the direction that Ferrell pointed. "Why'd you hide her in a box canyon?"

" 'Cause there's a dry steam bed filled with river rock flowin' out of it that covered our tracks. Maybe it wouldn't fool an Apache, but Milburn is no tracker and I doubt any of his boys are, either. Lilly was the only one that rode up in there. She's waiting on her sister. There's an old cabin hidden up at the end of the canyon and that's where Lilly is hiding."

Longarm pushed the horses into a trot and although the buckboard was a rough ride, he gritted his teeth and figured that they had better start making better time just in case a posse from Williams did suddenly appear.

Chapter 18

"This is where you get out and walk," Ferrell announced. "All you have to do is strike out for that box canyon. It isn't very deep. You'll see the old cabin in the trees."

Longarm reined in the horses and set the brake. "I'm going to take this real bad if Big Lips isn't up there. I'll come back and throw you in the Flagstaff jail."

"You'll find her. She's expectin' us to bring her sister along when all this fuss blows over."

"So how am I supposed to get us back to your ranch?"

"I don't know."

"You might need me when Milburn and his posse arrives."

"I don't think so. Me and the boys have a reputation for being able to take care of ourselves. They'll leave once they figure out that Big Lips Lilly isn't at my ranch. They might not be happy, but they'll go rather than risk a gunfight for nothing."

"And then you'll come get us?"

"Just as soon as it's clear," the old man promised.

Longarm didn't like the idea of hiking a mile or so across open grassland trying to leave no sign of his passing until he reached the box canyon. He liked even less

170

the idea that this crusty old codger might be pulling a slick one on him and sending him off into an empty box canyon. But Ferrell's reasoning was sound. If they drove the buckboard up into the canyon its tracks would be an open invitation for trouble.

"Okay," he said. "I'll see you soon."

"We won't come if there's any chance of us being watched by that Williams crowd."

"What about Irene?"

"I've decided we ought to just go ahead and bury her. It won't help Lilly to see her dead sister and you can tell her what you want about what happened. I don't envy you that, Marshal. Lilly knew that her sister was wild and sometimes on the crazy side, but she always had hope for her and they were close."

"Mind if I borrow that rifle you brought along?"

"Nope. I brought it for you. We don't want 'em to find and kill Lilly. It'd leave a real bad taste in all our mouths and we'd have to try and even the score with Milburn and his posse."

"I'll take care of her," Longarm promised as he turned and began to walk quickly across the grasslands.

He didn't look back until he was almost to the mouth of the canyon, and then he saw old man Ferrell climbing into the buckboard. Longarm figured that the cattleman had wiped out his tracks. Now, he just hoped that he would find Big Lips and manage to explain how her sister had died.

He was almost at the end of the mile deep canyon before he saw the little cabin hidden just below an outcropping of rock that jutted from the steep cliff. Longarm paused for a moment and turned, gazing back down into the valley. He really couldn't see much of it anymore, just a sliver because this canyon dog-legged to the right.

"Lilly!" he called. "Marshal Custis Long. I came to help you!"

His words echoed up and down the canyon walls. "Lilly! Your sister told me that she was the one that killed Governor Wilder. She said Wilder was cheating on you and she just couldn't take it anymore. She also told me that you *didn't* kill Judge Maxwell Otto."

Moments passed and his words echoed into silence. Longarm started forward, the rifle hanging loose in his left hand, his right hand near the gun on his hip. Cornered as she was right now, Big Lips might be just as crazy as her younger sister.

Suddenly, Big Lips stepped out from behind the trees just off to one side of the cabin. She had a pistol clenched in one hand and it was pointed down at Longarm. "Put your hands up high, Marshal."

"I came to help you."

"I've heard that before. How'd you find me?"

"Old man Ferrell brought me. He promised to come and get us when Milburn and his posse has come and gone."

"Drop the rifle and empty your holster with your left hand."

Longarm set the rifle down followed by his pistol.

"I don't blame you for being suspicious, but I'm here to protect, not arrest you."

"Maybe you are and maybe you aren't. I don't know yet. Let's walk over to the cabin, and I'll hear your story."

Longarm did as ordered, still wondering if he dared to tell Big Lips that her sister had died of a gunshot wound while they'd struggled on the ground beside the horse watering trough.

"Okay," Big Lips said, sitting down across from him on a log, but keeping her gun pointed in his general direction. "Let's hear it."

"Your sister confessed to killing Lance Wilder."

"That's a lie!"

"No," Longarm said, deciding he had no choice but to tell this woman everything. "Did you know that your sister was in Denver?"

"Sure. In fact," Big Lips said, "I was the one that urged her to go there in order not to be around when I was hanged."

"Well," Longarm said gently, "I met her in a blizzard in downtown Denver. She was being robbed and beaten by a couple of thugs. We were the only ones out on the street and I had to kill both men. After that, Irene and I became traveling companions on the train. She told me her name was Irene Hanson."

Big Lips smiled. "Irene was the best liar I ever knew. She could look a fella straight in the eye and tell him she loved him, then laugh the next day when she broke his heart. Did she break *your* heart, Marshal?"

"Not really. But I was sad when I learned she was the brains behind a plan to rob the train's vault. She found three loggers and, together, they took twenty-five thousand and a fair amount of gold."

"No!"

"I'm afraid it's true. She was going to pay old man Ferrell and his boys five thousand dollars after they sprang you from that boxcar up in Williams."

Big Lips shook her head. "Miles Ferrell is a good man and I always thought of him and his boys as friends, but I have to tell you that I was surprised when they risked so much by busting me out."

"He likes you, Lilly. But that wouldn't have been enough. Ferrell told me that he needed the money."

"He's got money already."

"Most folks can always find a use for another five thousand," Longarm told her. "And anyway, when we see him, he'll admit that what I've just told you is the truth."

"So Irene helped rob a train, huh?"

"That's right." Longarm decided there was no point in adding that a security guard had been murdered in the commission of the robbery. "Your sister thought a great deal of you."

"Damn fool! I love her, but she does do crazy things at times. Where is she?"

"At the Ferrell Ranch."

"We were going to run off together and live in Reno. Why didn't she come instead of you?"

"Because . . . because she couldn't." Longarm took a deep breath. "Lilly, I'm sorry to tell you this . . . but your sister is dead."

Big Lips almost fell off the log. Her face paled and she cocked back the hammer of her gun and pointed it at Longarm's heart, causing sweat to erupt across his forehead.

"You're lying to me!"

"I wish that I was, but I'm not. I was with her when she shot herself."

"No!"

"She admitted killing Wilder and she said that, having heard from you what the Yuma Prison was like, she couldn't stand to go there and she didn't think she could stand up to being sentenced to hang. So she . . . pulled the trigger of her own gun and died."

It was mostly the truth. Not all the truth, and he wasn't proud of it, but Longarm figured he could fill in the details later when Big Lips had time to get over her shock and initial grief. And when she wasn't pointing a cocked pistol at him.

Big Lips choked, "When did it happen?"

"Last night."

The gun sagged, now forgotten at the end the woman's arm. Longarm went over and took it away, then shoved the weapon in his empty holster and sat down beside Big Lips. "I'm very sorry."

174

"Damn," she whispered. "I knew that my sister was crazy and wasn't afraid of anything. And she's been in trouble with the law many times, but I never thought Irene would go so far as to help rob a train."

"She did it for you," Longarm said. "And she killed Wilder for the same reason. He was cheating on you."

"Hell, I knew that! I thought about killing him myself— more than once."

"Maybe Irene wanted to save you the trouble," Longarm told her. "She was a good sister, but what she did would have sent her straight to the gallows. In the end, she decided to confess the truth to me. But there's something that she wasn't quite able to tell me as she was dying."

Big Lips was staring at the dirt, dazed and in shock.

"Lilly," Longarm said, "did you hear me say that she wanted to tell me something but died trying?"

"What?" She started, eyes distant and unfocused.

"Your sister was trying to tell me who killed Judge Otto. She said it wasn't you, but she couldn't quite tell me who really did kill the judge."

Big Lips shook her head as if trying to rid herself of a nightmare. "Judge Otto?"

"Yes. Who killed him?"

She wiped her hands across her eyes as if to see a picture more clearly. "Stanton Pennington or his right hand man, Edward Westman, killed Judge Otto."

"Any proof?"

"No."

"Who is Edward Westman?"

Instead of answering, Big Lips swayed to her feet and then walked stoically into the cabin.

I'll give her a little time, Longarm thought, deciding to let the question ride. *And I'll tell her the whole truth when I think she's ready.*

• • •

Longarm went inside the darkening cabin as the sun began to fade behind the canyon walls. He found and lit a kerosene lamp, then pulled a crudely made stool up beside the bed where Big Lips lay staring up at the ceiling.

"Are you going to be all right?"

"Yeah."

"Anything I can get you?"

Big Lips spent a lot of time before answering. "There's a supply of passable whiskey in the cupboard over there by the stove. I could sure use a drink."

"Straight or with water?"

"Straight."

Longarm found several bottles of whiskey and a chipped coffee cup. He filled a glass and took it over to Big Lips, who sat up and nodded her thanks. She drank deeply and shook her head. "I'm really going to miss my sister. Most people thought Irene was a bad apple, but she had a lot of heart and she could be funny. My kid sister wasn't someone that you'd ever forget."

"No," Longarm agreed. "That's for sure."

Big Lips studied his face. "Did you sleep together on the train?"

"Yes."

"I thought so. Irene had a good eye for a man. She liked men, but, with one sad exception, never could bring herself to fully trust them. She had a few bad experiences when she was young. I tried to protect her heart but I couldn't. In the end, she turned out pretty cynical."

"I liked her." *Or at least*, Longarm thought, *I had until I discovered that almost everything she'd told me was a bald-faced lie.* "Irene had a lot of spirit."

"Exactly. Did she . . . die slow?"

"She died very quickly and not in pain."

"Thank heavens!" Big Lips came to her feet and took the cup from Longarm and refilled it to the brim. "When are we going to bury her?"

"She's already been buried."

"Couldn't they have waited for me?" she cried, almost dropping her glass.

"We all felt that it would be best not to do that. Your sister died wanting you to live. If we waited, the Williams posse might have arrived and caught you. There would have been a gunfight and a lot more people would have been killed needlessly. That's not what you'd have wanted, is it?"

"No," she said, voice dropping. Big Lips took another series of long, shuddering swallows. "So how long do we have to hide?"

"Only until after the posse is gone. Two, maybe three days at the most. Then Ferrell will show up and take us to his place where you can visit Irene's grave."

"All right." She refilled the cup again and handed it to Longarm. "Excuse me for my bad manners. Drink up, Marshal. I'm sure you weren't looking forward to any of this."

"No, I wasn't." Longarm drank and then said, "I don't think we can risk a fire in the stove tonight."

"That probably wouldn't be a very good idea," Big Lips agreed. "But it's going to get damn cold and there's only this warm old bearskin."

"I've got a coat and I'll manage."

"Are you hungry?"

"Some." Actually, Longarm was starving.

"We've got canned peaches and tomatoes and all the whiskey we can stomach."

"Then I reckon we will survive," he said. "Folks have gotten by on far less."

Big Lips nodded and found another cup. They went outside to sit on the log again and drank some more whiskey, watching the sunset over the mouth of the canyon.

Longarm was feeling the liquor but he still had that question on his mind. "Who is Edward Westman and why

177

did he or Stanton Pennington kill the judge?"

"Judge Otto was a blood-sucking leech who would do anything for money. My guess is that he must have found out something against Pennington and threatened to expose him. That would have prevented him from becoming governor."

"I see."

"And Westman?"

"He's Pennington's nephew and a lawyer from back east somewhere. They are both wildly ambitious. Pennington uses Westman to do his secret dirty work."

"Did your sister know this Edward Westman?"

Big Lips looked at him strangely. "Why do you ask?"

"Because she had someone help her in Prescott. And I need to know who that someone was because he must have most of the train robbery loot. And so I was wondering if it was this Westman fella. I think that Pennington used the word 'Edward' when he talked to his aide."

"I'm sure he did, so you've already met the man," Big Lips said. "Edward swept my sister off her feet when he first arrived in Arizona. He seemed nice and he was very charming and handsome. He was above her and myself. A prize, you might say. Anyway, he used Irene badly but she couldn't seem to give him up even though I told her to do so."

"Do you think she would have trusted him enough to have given him the train robbery money?"

Big Lips shrugged. "Maybe. Edward is smart and he's conniving. He had some power over my sister and he used it."

"Was there anyone else that your sister would have relied upon to help her?"

"No one but me."

Longarm decided that it was quite probably that the man who'd pistol-whipped him was, indeed, Edward Westman. And Westman was almost certainly the arrogant young aide that he'd met in the Governor's office. The one that had tried unsuccessfully to prevent him from interviewing Stanton Pennington until he'd used a bluff about the Secretary of State in Washington being on his side.

"The sun is almost down and it's getting cold. Let's go inside and open a few cans of peaches," Longarm said, noticing that Big Lips was starting to shiver.

After they ate the peaches and sat on the bed, Longarm said, "It is going to get cold tonight."

"You can sleep with me under the bearskin. But I don't want you to get the notion you can get romantic. I'm not in the mood tonight after hearing about Irene."

"I understand."

They drank a little more whiskey and with the air so cold in the old log cabin that they could see their breath, they both decided it was time to climb under the bearskin and get warm.

Longarm waited until Big Lips was under the bearskin and then he removed his boots and gun belt and climbed in beside her. She snuggled up close and laid her arm over his ribs. Moments later, she was fast asleep.

Well, he thought, this is a change of pace. But it's sure better than getting shot or freezing.

Longarm pulled the heavy rank-smelling bearskin up around his neck and soon fell asleep.

Chapter 19

They got snowed in for three days and while they had plenty of canned goods and whiskey, they grew hungry for fresh meat. So, Longarm and Big Lips went hunting when the weather cleared. Fortunately, on a bone-chilling afternoon, they shot a four-point buck down near the mouth of the canyon. They dressed it out and packed it back to the cabin and got a roaring fire going.

"No one is going to come looking for us in this foul weather," Longarm said. "And besides, I'm tired of freezing."

Lilly nodded in agreement. "We could go back under the bearskin while this place heats up."

"That might be nice."

Big Lips smiled. "Maybe you'd like to fool around a little this evening?"

"I've been wondering why they call you Big Lips. You're lips aren't especially big."

"Not the ones that you can see," she said coyly.

Longarm gulped and when the former madam began undressing, he was quick to follow her lead. Moments later, they were scrambling under the bearskin and madly groping for each other. She grabbed his manhood and when he wiggled his finger into her wet honey pot, he almost laughed. "My gosh, you've really got some big lips down there!"

He started to duck his head and peek, but she began French kissing and stroking him so vigorously that Longarm lost his curiosity and mounted the woman.

"Feel the difference?" she whispered.

"Yeah, I think so!" he panted.

"I've got a little more to work with than most women. So let's just enjoy ourselves and not talk anymore. Okay?"

"Whatever you say, Big Lips!"

Longarm had enjoyed a great many lovely women, but he couldn't remember ever being pleasured the way this one could pleasure. It seemed as if she able to milk him into a frenzy, then bring him back down again and again, each time higher and harder until he was about to go mad.

"Come on," she breathed into his ear. "We can keep this up a lot longer."

"Can we? I feel like I'm about to explode or got out of my mind."

"Just a little longer." Big Lips rolled him over and sat up, then slowly began to work his tool without moving any visible part of her lovely body. "What do you think about this?"

"Who needs to think? I can feel what you're doing! And I don't know how you do it, but don't stop."

Big Lips laughed and kept working him higher and higher. Longarm's testicles felt as if they were the size of melons and they ached with a sweet but incredibly intense pleasure. He could see that she was starting to quiver and reach her own joyous peak, and when Big Lips suddenly threw back her head, bucked and howled, he knew she was in the delicious throes of her own ecstasy.

Longarm grabbed the woman by her hips and lost his senses filling her with torrents of his seed. Torrents that went on and on until even his mouth went dry.

Big Lips collapsed on top of him, and they lay panting and fighting for breath until she moaned, "Let it snow and snow, honey. I want to stay right here and keep doin' it over and over!"

Longarm felt so depleted that he wasn't entirely sure that he could keep doing it to Big Lips . . . at least not that way. Why, he was drained as dry as a seedless desert gourd and when he climbed to his feet to cut some venison for the fire, his legs even felt a little shaky.

"You're a fine specimen of manhood," Big Lips said, leaning on one elbow and eyeing him with appreciation. "We're going to have some wild times before this storm passes! You ever done the Chinese Corkscrew to a woman?"

"What's that?"

"Come back over here and I'll show you. It'll make you wish your head was screwed down tighter so you won't blow your mind."

"Well, listen, it sounds interesting, but we need some red meat."

"I just had some, Big Lover Boy." The woman pointed to his dangling member and laughed coarsely. That got Longarm to thinking that it might be best if the weather soon cleared.

When Miles Ferrell and three of his sons finally managed to reach their cabin two days later, Longarm was sore and exhausted. He'd never known a woman with such an insatiable appetite for lovemaking. Under the bearskin, on top of the bearskin and even *through* the rotting and mangy old bearskin. Why, Big Lips, with her unusual anatomy seemed as if she could do it all night and all day without ever getting enough satisfaction.

"You look like you've had a hard time here," the old rancher said when he first saw Longarm standing half bent in the cabin's doorway.

"I have."

But Big Lips shook her head. "We've just been having some good old down home fun. Know what I mean?"

"Yeah," the rancher said. "I remember what you mean. You ready to get back to the ranch?"

"Sure!" Longarm said, perhaps with more enthusiasm than was justified. "Did Milburn and his Williams posse show up?"

"Yep. And they were damned mad when I let them have a look around and they couldn't find Big Lips. He threatened me and the boys but I don't think nothing will come of it."

Longarm was relieved. And when they got back to the old man's cattle ranch, he wasted no time in asking for a change of clothes.

"You and Big Lips do sort of smell fishy," one of the Ferrell men offered. "I can't quite figure out exactly what you both do smell like."

"It's that bearskin," Longarm said quickly. "It was pretty rank."

"I shot him myself," the old rancher bragged. "Killed that big bastard about twenty years ago. Pretty fine pelt, huh?"

"It's had its time," Longarm answered. "Now, I'm going into Prescott and seeing if I can get some answers."

"I want to go with you," Big Lips said, looking subdued because she'd just been out to visit her sister's fresh grave. "I need to put an end to the idea that it was me that killed Judge Otto. And the only way that will happen is to get a confession either from Stanton Pennington or his young aide and nephew, Edward Westman."

"The Governor won't confess anything," Ferrell said. "He's too tough. But you might break that young aide of his if you play your cards right."

Longarm nodded with agreement. And besides, if Edward had used Irene, then he was the one that would have

183

the stolen gold and cash. Fresh hundred dollar bills whose serial numbers ought to have been recorded at the Denver Mint.

Longarm and Big Lips waited almost two days before they had the opportunity to catch Edward Westman working alone in the Governor's offices. The handsome young attorney had stayed late and when he saw Longarm and Big Lips, Westman must have sensed he was trapped because he lunged for his desk and tried to tear open the upper drawer.

Longarm struck Edward in the side of his jaw and dropped him unconscious to the floor. Opening the drawer, he found a pistol and an envelope containing a thousand dollars in uncirculated one hundred dollar bills.

"Get some water," he told Big Lips.

"You're thirsty?"

"No. I'm going to wake him up and present him with some evidence that even a lawyer couldn't deny."

When Big Lips returned, Longarm poured the cup of water over Westman's face, rousing the man. Then Longarm knelt beside the lawyer, and with the wad of fresh bills in one of his fists and his gun in the other, Longarm said, "It's confession time. I've got the evidence I need to see you convicted of murder."

"Murder!"

"That's right. A security guard on the train where this money was taken was killed. You've got the money and that makes you an accessory to murder." Longarm knew he needed more ammunition so he ran another bluff by saying, "Furthermore, we have an eyewitness that will testify that he saw *you* kill Judge Otto."

"No!" the still groggy young man protested. "I didn't kill him. The Governor did! Sure, I was there but. . . ."

Perhaps Edward Westman's senses returned in a rush because he suddenly clamped his mouth shut.

"It doesn't matter if you talk anymore or not," Longarm said, dragging the man to his feet. "Because we're going to get the rest of the money and then we're going to jail."

"That's all I've got!"

"Where is the rest of it?"

"It's in Stanton's office safe."

"Do you know the combination?"

"Sure," Westman stammered, "but. . . ."

Longarm shoved the young lawyer toward the door. "Let's go to his office and you can open the safe up."

"Why should I do that?"

"Because," Longarm said, "I'm the only one who can recommend that the witness tell the truth and change his story to admit that he didn't see you kill Judge Otto."

Westman considered that response carefully, then said, "If I agree to sign a written confession naming Governor Stanton Pennington as the one that killed Judge Otto, will you vouch for my credibility?"

"I might."

"Marshal, that's not good enough and you know it."

"Why did Pennington kill judge Otto?"

"Because Otto had some goods on him. Something to do with illegal use of public funds. The Governor asked me to 'take care of the problem' but when I realized that meant murder, I refused."

"But you did go with him to kill Judge Otto."

"I . . . I went hoping to talk some sense into *both* of them. Otto was being greedier than usual and Stanton was . . . well, he was insane with rage at the idea of being blackmailed. But when they got together, things just got worse and that's when Stanton killed Judge Otto. I swear I didn't do it!"

Longarm believed the young man, but he wanted to test him just to make sure. "Are you the one who hit me in the back of the head when I was standing across the street from the Pink Lady Saloon?"

Westman lowered his eyes. "Yeah. I also helped Irene get you into the buckboard and out of town."

"All right," Longarm said. "I believe you. Let's get the stolen money and gold, then go back to your office where you'll write a confession."

It took nearly an hour to get everything in order and even less time to arrest the outraged territorial governor and escort him to a jail cell beside that of his young but obviously repentant aide.

"Marshal Butrum," Longarm said to the sleepy, half-dressed lawman who had been summoned from the hotel where he roomed. "You're relieved of your duties until further notice."

The marshal, a slovenly sort, blustered and ranted until Longarm grabbed him by the nape of his neck and propelled him out the door and into the street. And while Longarm stood guard and waited for dawn, Big Lips Lilly Cameron sent a telegraph to Denver asking for more federal assistance.

"Wait for a reply no matter how long it takes," he told Big Lips. "We've landed a big fish and we're going to need some assistance."

"Are we both going to have to stay in that pigpen of a marshal's office until help arrives?"

"I'm afraid so. It's as much for your protection as my own. There are still some people out there who might think you're fair game and worthy of a bounty. One of them would be John Milburn, who would love to arrest you again and get his name in the headlines."

Big Lips understood. "Well," she said, "I guess we'll just have to make the best of things. I'll get some rolls of canvas along with extra food and bedding."

"I understand the extra food and bedding," Longarm said with puzzlement, "but what's the use for canvas?"

"Well," Big Lips said, shaking her ample bosom and

giving him a lascivious wink that left no doubt as to her bawdy intentions, "we don't want them to *watch* us improve on the old Chinese Corkscrew . . . do we, honey?"

For one of the rare times in his life, Longarm was so surprised that he couldn't think of an answer.

Watch for

LONGARM AND THE OZARK ANGEL

283rd novel in the exciting LONGARM series
from Jove

Coming in June!